NO PROOF

ASHLEY MCCONNELL

To my readers:

I'm sorry about the cliff-hanger.

Ha, no, not really. That brought me a lot of joy.

NO PROOF

COUGHED, AND A SANGUINE TASTE DANCED ON MY LIPS. I had enough energy to slide my left hand down to my abdomen; it was wet. I shivered uncontrollably, the leaves crunching beneath my back. My barely-clothed body lying in the open amongst the trees, leaves cascading down, surrounding me.

When a tree sheds its leaves, the leaf dies. How ironic that I lay here, dying, amongst them.

PROLOGUE

CHAPTER 1

Sadie

I HEARD THE FRONT DOOR OPEN AND GLANCED UP AT THE clock on the microwave; six o'clock. Right on time. Ben, my boyfriend of four years, was home from work and dinner was just about done. Today was our fourth anniversary, so I made his favorite—a cast iron skillet seared steak served medium rare, a baked potato with homemade bacon bits, green beans, and fresh garlic toast. Even though I knew it was his favorite, I'd be lying if I said it wasn't mine as well.

Ben's footsteps got closer, and as he turned the corner, entering our stark white kitchen, his jacket was still hanging off his broad shoulders, and his shoes were still on.

"Planning on staying a while?" I tried to ask playfully, but I couldn't control my freshly penciled-in eyebrow from raising.

"Sadie, can we sit down on the couch, please?" His voice was firm . . . was he about to propose?

I had been dropping hints for over a year; as soon as we

moved in together, I started casually leaving my laptop open when I would leave the room, hoping he would notice the wedding websites I was perusing. My goal wasn't to pressure him into proposing but rather to show that I was ready to take the next step in our relationship. We had some rough patches during our relationship, but what couple hadn't?

The last time we spoke about it was just over ten months ago at his company's Christmas party. He'd had a few too many cocktails and I'd had close to an entire bottle of Champagne. It was a tipsy conversation in the Uber on the way home and might have carried no weight for Ben, but for me, I took his drunk words as his sober thoughts. Maybe this was what he wanted to sit down and talk about.

We walked to the couch and sat down. Ben immediately started speaking, "Look, I know this might seem out of the blue, but I think it's best that we end things. I've not been happy for a while, and well, I've found someone else." He reached for my hand, but I quickly pulled it back, hugging it to my chest. "Someone I want to grow old with."

I stared at him, mouth agape, unsure what to say. I felt like a knife was just plunged into my chest and twisted. Was this a joke? It had to be.

"This isn't funny, Ben." My palms were sweaty. I wiped them on my jeans.

"I wish I were joking, but I'm not."

"So you chose today to do this?" My voice went up an octave, cracking on the last word.

I was met with a blank stare—not an ounce of recognition in his deep, ocean-blue eyes. "You don't even know what today is, do you?"

His knee started to bounce, and he ran a hand through his chestnut hair; I could tell he didn't remember that today was our anniversary. All of the blood in my body came to the surface and I could feel the hammering in my chest.

"I'll take that as a no. It's September 18." I paused, giving him a moment to remember, "Our fourth anniversary."

Not wanting to sit near him, I moved back to my perch by the stove, flipping the steaks one last time before turning off the burner. I watched a wave of realization fall over his face. "Sadie, look . . ."

Ben walked over to where I was in the kitchen and said, "I'm sorry that this is how things have to end for us, but I hope you end up happier with someone else. We've not been that way for a while. I think you know that."

Hot tears pricked at the corners of my eyes when I said, "I think the unhappiness might have been one-sided"—I inhaled sharply—"because *this* is news to me."

"I know this is hard, but I'll need you moved out by the end of the weekend."

"As in two days from now?"

"Yes, you don't have much, so it shouldn't take long, right?"

Was he serious? Not only was he breaking up with me, but he was kicking me out with nowhere to go.

"I have my clothes, some furniture, my books, and—"

Ben cut me off, "Well, I paid for most of the furniture, so I'll be keeping that."

I didn't care that the tears were spilling over. "You're kidding me! We each paid for half of everything in this house. By that logic, I should be taking *half of everything.*"

"I figured you could go back home and live with your parents so that you wouldn't need much more than your clothes and stupid books."

Oh, he went there.

"You're a real piece of work, Ben Thomson. I hope you and your new 'love' are very happy together." It took every ounce of

3

my strength not to lunge at his throat. Not only was he kicking me out, but he was also condescending about it. I turned off all the stove burners and went into the hall closet to get my suitcase. I intentionally took the long way to the bedroom, rolling it on the floors more than I needed to, something that bugged the shit out of him for whatever reason. I ripped the drawers open, throwing clothes in my suitcase.

"Sadie, wait, let's finish this conversation."

I spun on my heel. "There's nothing else to say. When you decided to toss this in the mix, did you think I would want to sit down and converse with you?"

"I mean, yeah. You love me; don't you want to know why I don't love you?"

How in the world did I give this man four precious years of my life?

"Ben! Fucking stop while you're ahead." The tears were streaming down my face quicker than they ever had before. I wasn't sure what was worse—getting dumped on your anniversary or your ex-boyfriend standing there, wanting to list off reasons why he doesn't love you anymore.

He shrugged, obviously understanding that it wasn't the best thing to say. "I'm going to head out; text me when you're done. Can I hug you?"

"You *must* be stupid." I pointed in the direction of the front door.

He nodded and walked out of the bedroom. I heard the front door close softly, and I looked around the house as I sat down on the bed; a bomb had just been dropped into my life. I wasn't going to let the dinner I had worked so hard on go to waste, so I made a plate for myself and ate in silence at the kitchen counter. I texted my mom to let her know what had happened and that they should be expecting me. I grabbed my travel tote and headed to the bathroom to gather up my toiletries, catching a glimpse of my reflection in the mirror. My mascara was running down my flushed cheeks, my blue eyes were glassy, and the skin around them was puffy.

A chapter in my life closed tonight, one that I wasn't ready to end. Where would I go? What would I do now?

CHAPTER 2

Sadie

"**Y**OU'RE GOING TO LOVE THIS UNIT, THE NEIGHBORS are fantastic, and it gets amazing light in the main bedroom in the morning," Linda, the community leasing agent, mentioned as we walked up to 807 Blue Sky Avenue. I nodded, both excited and terrified to be looking at this home for rent. Excited because this was a fresh start for me but terrified because I'd never lived alone before. I lived at my parents' house throughout college to save money, and when I graduated, I moved in with Ben.

"This is a two-bedroom, two-bathroom townhome—many tenants use the other bedroom as a home gym, but I've also seen it used as an office, something you might want to consider since you work from home." Linda tucked a strand of her long, strawberry-blonde hair behind her ear as she unlocked the door. "Even though your unit is sandwiched between two, it's a beautiful open-concept floor plan, with lots of natural light. You'll see when we get inside." The lock clicked open and she said, "Here we are, go on in!"

I walked through the door, amazed at what I saw. The kitchen was spacious and furnished with gray cabinets and the most beautiful white marble countertop with a massive black vein running through it. The floors were natural wood, stained a deep gray—one shade darker than the cabinets. What would be my bedroom was enormous; the bathroom was stunning and furnished in the same color palette as the kitchen. The second bedroom was smaller but would make for a great office space with windows to allow for people-watching while I worked and, Linda was right, lots of natural light. This was everything I wanted in a house, never mind a rental.

I walked into the pantry, flicked the light, and checked it out. "You said this complex allows pets, correct?" One of the main reasons I wanted to live here was because I wanted to adopt a dog.

She nodded. "It's $20 per month on top of the base rent." Linda stayed in the dining room area, giving me space to walk around and check everything out. "Do you have a pet?"

"No, not yet. I'm hoping to adopt a dog soon, though." I smiled warmly at her.

"I'm not married and have two dogs; they've been my best decisions. It's so nice to have wagging tails that welcome you when you get home. One of my pups brings me a toy every time I walk through the door as a welcome home present; it doesn't matter if I've only been gone fifteen minutes; he's always waiting for me."

I laughed softly at the personal anecdote; that was exactly what I was looking for—another living being in my house to brighten it up and be excited when I got home. Surely that was a thing, replace a stupid relationship with a loving dog?

I walked around again, checking out the small fenced-in backyard, imagining a warm summer afternoon with a dog playing and me sitting in a hammock, reading a book. I took the place in once more before turning to Linda and announcing, "I think I'm ready to head back to the leasing office."

"Let's head on back!" Linda locked up the unit and we walked back to the office, which seemed like more of a formality, as I had every intention of applying on the spot. Once back, Linda went to her desk and said, "Here's my card. If you have any questions, please—"

Before she could even get the words out, I blurted out, "I'd like to apply! It checked all the boxes of things I was looking for."

Her eyebrows shot up, telling me this wasn't a regular occurrence "Oh! Okay then, the computers are right over there." She pointed through some glass doors to a small business center with two computers, a smaller conference table, and a very out-of-date printer. I sat down, filling out the application in record time. Since I didn't have a place to live at the moment, I needed this application approved yesterday.

I wasn't technically homeless—I'd spent the last few nights at my parents' house. After the break-up, I ate my dinner, packed up his and took it with me (yes, I know it's petty), threw all my stuff in various boxes and bags, and after a few trips, I'd successfully dumped it all in the middle of my parents' living room. I knew they didn't mind having me back in the house for a few days, but it was certainly not a permanent solution. No one wants to live as a late twenty-something in their childhood bedroom. My parents never found another use for the room, and as an only child, I thought that they would have turned it into a home gym or something after I moved out a few years ago, but no, they left it as it was. It still had posters of Zac Efron and Taylor Swift from 2007 on the closet doors; this wasn't sustainable—it was the cool thing to do then, but it just felt creepy now. I loved my parents, but I needed to be out and on my own, not relying on others anymore.

I left Linda and returned to the house, ready to send over three months' worth of paystubs and not-so-patiently reflect on the string of decisions that led me to this point: Sitting on the green and white floral sofa I grew up with, watching Saturday morning cartoons.

This new place would be my sanctuary, and I would finally take ownership of my happiness. My entire life, I was sheltered and given whatever I wanted, so material things brought me joy. As I got older, my teenage friends brought more substance to my life. Then, when I graduated college and moved in with Ben, I based my entire existence on him and what *he* enjoyed. I never did things I wanted to do; I always accommodated others. If my friends wanted to go see a horror movie, I would never rain on their parade and tell them that I was too chicken. I would just suck it up and go, then wouldn't sleep for days because it had scared me half to death.

If Ben wanted to go out to get Greek food, I would happily oblige, even though Greek food was my least favorite type of cuisine. Just the thought of a Gyro made me sick. I would still go and have a small salad, not that he would notice my plate was still half full when the waiter returned to drop off the check. That would require him to care about someone other than himself. I saw that now in hindsight.

Our entire relationship hadn't always been bad—it started well, and both of us were young and madly in love. Then he started working and got busy; he threw himself into his career, not caring who he hurt or got fired in his path, as long as it made him look better. When he started traveling for work more frequently, I was initially lonely but came to appreciate how it felt to live alone. I was more relaxed, and most importantly, I could watch whatever I wanted on television. At this point in my life, I'd been living to make everyone else happy, putting my wants, needs, and desires on the back burner. So now, aside from reading to escape my reality, I didn't know what made *me* happy anymore. Who was Sadie Augustine? Maybe this breakup was a blessing in disguise.

It took twenty-four hours for my renter's application to be approved. As soon as I saw that email in my inbox, I loaded everything into my car and my dad's truck and was off to get my keys. I met Linda at the leasing office, and she handed everything to me—keys, garage door opener, and a welcome packet with a goodie bag. I drove to my unit and pulling into the driveway felt like coming home.

As silly as it was, I bought a wreath for the front door; it was the least I could do to make it feel like mine. I walked up to the front door and turned the key in the lock, opening the door to my new beginning. I hung up the wreath and went inside; at that moment, I realized that I had quite the feat ahead of me, but I was ready for the expensive challenge. I had no furniture except for a bookshelf and a random coffee table, absolutely no food, and no mattress, so I was going to have to do my best to make it through. I unpacked my clothes and my few housewares and set up the air mattress I borrowed from my parents, making it both my bed and couch.

One major perk about this house was that the Internet was already set up, so I just had to activate it. I ordered some Chinese food and went to my bedroom to sit on my makeshift couch and watch some episodes of *Friends*. This was my first night living alone, and I was more anxious than I had anticipated. With the help of my comfort show, Hershey kisses, and all the lights on, I finally fell asleep around two-thirty until the sun popped over the horizon and woke me up at seven.

Lacking all motivation but in desperate need of furniture, I started my day. The furniture store opened at nine, and I planned on being there when they opened so they could take all my money, and then head to the grocery store to fill my barren fridge. To be honest . . . there was something so freeing about living on your own; there was no one there to tell you to put on pants, or to scowl at you when you ate ice cream for dinner, or even better when you just wanted to sit and do nothing. It felt like even though my heart was shattered into a million pieces a week ago when Ben walked out the door, I would be just fine on my own. I was intelligent, a business owner, and a badass.

I got ready for the day, tossed my hair in a bun on the top of my head, and swiped on some mascara. It wouldn't be a proper morning without a run to the local coffee shop, so I stopped there first and then set out to the furniture store. We didn't have any furniture stores in Red Oak, so I had to drive over to the next city to begin this process. Today was going to be a long day, so this coffee was my savior. I pulled into the parking lot and sat there momentarily, bracing myself. I knew this wouldn't be easy because the last time I was in this store, Ben and I had picked out furniture together. I inhaled sharply and headed toward the entrance.

Walking in, I was immediately overwhelmed; I knew what style I liked, but there was just so much that I didn't know where to begin. I must have looked like a deer in headlights because a saleswoman came over to help.

"Good morning. Are you looking for anything in particular today?" I looked at her name tag, Emily. She was older and had kind green eyes and seemed like she genuinely wanted to help me, not just make a commission.

"Hey, good morning! I need everything."

Her eyebrows perked up. "Such as?"

"When I say everything, I mean *everything*. I need a bedroom set, mattress, dining room set, couch, television stand, desk . . . the list goes on and on."

"How fun! First-time homeowner?" I didn't correct her. I knew she was being friendly, but at that moment, the reality of the situation hit, and it felt like a ton of bricks landed on my chest. I felt a panic attack coming, my first one in years. My palms were sweaty, my heart raced, my ears rang, my mind went fuzzy, and it felt as though all the oxygen had been sucked out of the building. I was on the verge of passing out.

"Ma'am, you look a little pale; why don't we go sit down." It wasn't a question; it was more of a demand. Emily led me to the living room section of the store and sat me down on the most comfortable couch. Amidst my panic, in typical Sadie fashion, I glanced at the price tag—I'd be getting it. I focused on my breathing while Emily ran over to the break room. She sprinted back over to me with a granola bar and a water bottle in her hands.

"Please drink some water. One of the associates is on his way with some juice to help with your blood sugar. Are you hungry? Do you suffer from low blood sugar?"

I shook my head, still unable to calm myself down enough to get words out. I took some deep breaths and remembered what my therapist had told me all those years ago, "*Breathe in through your nose and slowly exhale through your mouth.*" I did that a few more times before it started to help; the world became clearer, and I could get some words out.

"I'm so sorry, that was a panic attack. I've not had one in years."

"Are you okay now? Is there anyone I can call for you?"

"No, I'll be all right, thank you."

"If you're sure. Why don't we sit here, get you feeling better, and discuss what you need for your house? Do you have any pictures of the space or anything you had in mind?"

Since Emily mentioned it, perusing Pinterest before coming here would have probably been a good idea because while I knew what I didn't like, I had no clue how to match the pieces

I did like. As much as I was gifted with the ability to design a killer logo, interior design was not within my skill set.

"I can show you the floor plan, but I don't have any inspirational pictures. I like clean and classic. Nothing that will go out of style and nothing that will show wear and tear, I want to be able to keep these pieces for years and have them still look new." I handed over my phone for her to take a look.

"Do you live alone, or do you have kids or pets?"

"I . . . live alone as of last night. No kids, no pets."

"Oh, sweetie, I'm so sorry."

I nodded, refusing to make eye contact. "Yeah, a sudden break-up has led me here. He insisted on keeping everything we had."

"What an asshole!" Emily slapped a hand over her mouth. "I'm so sorry. That was unprofessional."

I laughed at her candor. "Nothing to apologize for; you're spot on."

"You're looking a little less pale. Did you want to start talking about the furniture?"

"Yes, please. Can we start with this couch? It's amazing." I rubbed my hand along the smooth fabric.

"Did you see that it reclines?" She pushed a button on the side of the couch, and the whole seat reclined. Now as I lay down, I could feel my body relax and was even more sold on this couch.

"Let's add this to my list; can we plan around it?"

"Absolutely. Did you have a budget in mind?" She paused then said, "I'm sorry, with all the excitement, I didn't catch your name."

"I made quite the entrance, didn't I? I'm Sadie, it's nice to meet you." I couldn't muster a huge smile, but a small one danced on my lips.

"Likewise!" Emily jotted down my name and the item

number of the couch, and we started walking around, picking out all the necessary pieces to furnish my new home. With each piece I picked, I started to feel better—I could do this on my own.

It took two weeks and nearly draining my savings account to furnish this place, but my furniture was delivered and put together, and it looked pretty damn good, if I did say so myself. Since the floors and cabinets were gray, I opted for driftwood-colored furniture to tie everything together. I picked pale blues and greens, aiming to make it serene, taking color palette inspiration from a Californian spa I'd been to with my mom a few years back. Slowly but surely, I made my home into my safe space. I might have been surrounded by predominantly fifty-plus couples, but it felt safe here, like nothing bad could ever happen because, why would it? Nothing ever happened in the town of Red Oak—we were a lackluster group.

This apartment complex had everything I could have ever dreamed of: Heated, in-ground pool, a jacuzzi, two dog parks, and a massive green space which was the perfect spot to bring a blanket, snacks, and a book and spend the afternoon. I hadn't even mentioned the best part—being in a community; the leasing office hired a company to come and plow the streets and sidewalks when it snowed, which, in Vermont, was often. Did you know that Vermont received more snow yearly than any other state? If you Googled it, you'd see—on average, we got fifty-four days of snow, which equated to 89.25 inches. To put that timeframe into perspective, that would be as if it snowed every day from January 1st until February 24th. It was insanity, but when you'd lived here your entire life, you were used to it by now.

Red Oak, Vermont, was merely a blip on the map, but it was something special. I could drive by and see where I went on my first date, where I fell out of the tree and broke my ankle, or visit the house where I grew up. While most of my classmates left Vermont the first chance they got, I didn't; I stuck around because this was where my life was. My parents and grandparents were here, and my best friend, Audrey.

Now that I'd been settled for a month, I was lonely. I knew it would take some getting used to, but the silence in this house was maddening. Being left to your thoughts when you were a chronic overthinker was a slippery slope to insanity; the number of panic attacks I'd had since moving in said so.

I sat down on my new reclining leather couch, propped my laptop against the armrest, and started my search for dogs that were available for adoption. I started at the local shelter and on the top of the page was a beautiful Golden Retriever puppy named Melody, just twelve weeks old. My heart shattered when I read her story. She and her mom were found on the side of the road, scared and alone. Who would do this to these sweet babies? I read further; her mom was adopted last week, and the pup was left in the shelter alone and had been crying for her ever since.

I didn't need to look any further; I knew this little girl would be the perfect addition to my quiet home. I could provide the love and shelter she desperately needed. I read more about the process—I'd have to fill out the application, then if I were approved, they would do a home study and bring the dog to meet me. I filled out the application and crossed my fingers, opening Pinterest to save some ideas for at-home dog treats. I told myself years ago when Ben and I were initially talking about getting a dog, that I would be the person who made all their dog treats. I'd want nothing but the best for my new housemate.

I closed my laptop and checked my email, looking to see when the shelter would potentially be getting back to me: it said the application would be reviewed within forty-eight hours. It was Saturday, so I knew the forty-eight-hour window would be more like seventy-two. I spent the rest of the weekend running errands and going to a spa with Audrey for a very much-needed massage and facial. Audrey and I had been inseparable since we were three. We went to the same preschool and the rest is history. The longer we'd been friends, the more like sisters we'd become.

When Monday rolled around, I had put the adoption out of my mind, so when my phone rang at ten in the morning and it was a number I didn't recognize on the screen, I was surprised.

"Hello, this is Sadie."

"Hi, Sadie! This is Anita with Vermont Animal Rescue. How are you doing today?"

My pulse sped up, and I sat up straighter in my desk chair as I said, "I'm doing well, thank you. How are you?"

"I'm good, thanks for asking! I was calling about your application for Melody. Is now a good time to chat? This won't take very long—I only need maybe ten minutes."

I clicked save on the logo I was working on and moved to the sofa in my office to remove all potential distractions. "Yes, it is!"

"Great! This call's purpose is to validate all the information in your application."

It took five minutes to review all my basic information.

"So, the next steps are for us to call your references and if that all checks out, then we'll go ahead and do a home study and have you meet Melody."

"That sounds great, I look forward to hearing from you!"

We hung up, and I could not focus on my work for the day; I was too distracted by the fact that the shelter was calling my mom,

Audrey, and one of my good friends from college. Two hours later, my phone rang again, the same number from earlier.

"Sadie! It's Anita again—I have good news! Your application has been approved, and your references checked out. Are you available for us to come by this week and just check everything out? That would be the last step in the process."

"That's wonderful news. Yes, I'll be home all week."

"Any days or times that work best for you?"

"I work from home, so I have open availability."

"Oh, that's even better; she'll get lots of attention then. Are you free later today?"

"Wow, that's quick." I couldn't hide my surprise. "Yes. I have a client call until 3:30, but I'm free after that."

"I'm assuming you don't have dog supplies yet, correct?"

"No, ma'am. I didn't want to buy anything until I knew what dog I would adopt."

"Okay, let's plan on us coming over around six, does that work for you? Hopefully, that will give you enough time to get everything you'll need for the first night."

"That sounds great. I'm excited to meet her!"

"See you then!" And the line went dead.

My new dog was going to be here by the end of the day, and I had absolutely nothing prepared for her. I grabbed the notepad and pen off my desk and started a list of things I needed to get this afternoon. While I was deep in my list-making, my work email chimed. It was my afternoon client asking to move our call to next week. I shifted the meeting as requested, and now the rest of my day was wide open.

I wrapped up some final edits on a logo design and called it a day at 2 p.m. I started my mission at the pet supplies store, getting almost everything I needed, then headed to Walmart to get the remaining items. As soon as I got home, I started setting everything up for . . . a name. I had forgotten to think of a name. I was already failing at this dog mom thing.

I set up her beds (yes, I bought two—one for the bedroom and one for my office) and got her box of toys situated. I looked around my house and somehow, it already felt like more life had been breathed into it. The next few hours felt like five years, which was overly dramatic but true. I occupied my time by getting ahead on some work, and before I knew it, the doorbell was ringing.

I opened it to find a wide-smiling Anita and an itty bitty puppy hiding behind her feet, poking half of her head out. I greeted Anita, shook her hand, and then crouched down to the puppy's level.

"Hi there." I stuck my flat hand out, allowing the dog to sniff it and understand that I wasn't a threat.

"You can pet her, she might be a little bit skeptical."

With that permission granted, I reached over and scratched her little fuzzy head. "Oh, you're just the sweetest baby, aren't you?" The puppy's tail started wagging like crazy.

"Be careful you might take off!" I already had the annoying dog mom voice nailed down.

"She's a big fan of yours already," Anita observed.

"And I'm a fan of hers too. Why don't you both come on in?" I stood up and moved out of the doorway, allowing them to enter.

"I would recommend closing any doors to spaces she wouldn't be allowed in."

"She's going to have free reign of this place." I sat down cross-legged on the floor. "I can stay with her and play if you want to look around? The back door is open, so you can go check out the yard."

"Sounds good! You two have fun."

I grabbed a small stuffed bunny from the toy box and handed it to her. She grabbed it immediately, and instead of taking it elsewhere to chew it, she crawled into my lap and snuggled up with it. She was all I needed. I zoned out while petting her because the next thing I knew, Anita was standing above me.

"What are you going to name her?" she asked, clipboard in hand.

"I . . . I hadn't thought of one. I was hoping if I saw her, a name would just come to mind that described her perfectly."

"Do you mind?" She motioned to the couch.

"Please, have a seat."

"Not everyone has a name picked out. Why don't you tell me some of your favorite things, and we can see if there's anything to work with?" Anita was scribbling on the sheet of paper, presumably filling out the home study form.

"I like pizza, reading, chocolate, Jane Austen, and flowers."

"What is your favorite flower?"

"Daisies."

Anita looked down at the puppy snuggled up in my lap with her little stuffed bunny and announced, "I think she looks like a Daisy. What do you think, sweet girl?" She tickled the dog's stomach, and her tail went crazy.

"She seems to like it," I observed.

"So, Daisy, it is?"

"Daisy, it is." I stroked her little cheek and thought, *We're going to be the best of friends. Daisy.* Her soft golden coat and one brown eye, one blue eye were just some of the things that I loved about her.

I signed on the dotted line and we were on our own, just like that.

PRESENT

CHAPTER 3

Sadie

I WAS ONE OF THOSE PEOPLE WHO ENJOYED THE SNOW WHEN I was indoors, but when it was time to go outside, I questioned all of my life's decisions that led me to that point. I was born and raised in Vermont, so I didn't know life any other way. There was always so much snow that I learned recipes off YouTube for different ice creams, sorbets, and frozen cocktails once I was old enough. Today, a margarita made with my favorite tequila, some fresh snow from my front yard, and lime juice was making the gloominess outside my window a little more bearable. March was always the longest month with the most snow here.

Today's snow wasn't a fresh one, all white and pretty; it was three days post-snowstorm. So, the streets were covered in a black slush, the curbs piled high with yellow snow, the sidewalks were constantly wet and covered with salt, and the world just looked cold and gray. I stared out the slightly frost-covered window over my desk that looked straight to the front yard. Work was finished up for the week, so this margarita was my reward for making it through.

I had turned the spare bedroom in the front of the house into my dream office but added a sleeper sofa so I could offer out-of-town family and friends a place to stay. I'd picked up a white wooden desk to contrast against the walls and floor, added a beautiful navy blue rug, the deep navy sleeper sofa, and two bookcases for either side of my desk, so they bordered the window. The rest of the house was great, but this was my favorite spot—it was the most 'Sadie.'

I shifted from my desk chair to the sofa, placing my frosty glass on a coaster on the metal end table and putting my feet up. I reached for my newly-purchased thriller with zero intentions of moving for many hours. My plan was to start and finish the book this evening. I dove in, immersing myself in the fictional world the author had superbly created. I'd barely gotten lost in the story before what little daylight there was began rapidly fading, so I flicked on the end table lamp and continued reading for a few more hours. My stomach growled, and I was at a good stopping point in the book, so I heated some of last night's leftover broccoli and cheddar soup and moved to the living room to watch some television. As I was getting up, something caught my eye out the window—it looked like a moving truck; my next-door neighbors were moving out. I felt the corners of my mouth droop slightly; I'd enjoyed their company over the last two years—the couple moved in just about a year after I did, and we hit it off immediately. I always felt secure living next to them; the husband was retired from the Army and always kept an eye on my unit. I didn't envy them, though; moving in the winter was not a fun task, especially in the snowiest state in the country. I made a mental note to stop by tomorrow and say goodbye, wish them well on their move.

This week had me exhausted. Something about the frigid air made you want to go back to bed and sleep for days. With my original plan of reading all night thwarted, when the movie I opted for was over, my eyelids were heavy, so I let Daisy out one last time for the night, and then we went to bed. Usually, I was up until after midnight, but it was only nine-thirty tonight when I fell into bed, turned on an episode of *Friends*, snuggled up with Daisy, and drifted off to sleep.

I could see the morning sun peeking through the blinds, so I knew today was my opportune chance to run all my errands for the week. I snuggled back in the blankets, picking up my phone and checking what was going on in the world. Not five minutes later, Daisy jumped up on the bed, clearly ready to start her day. I took this as my sign. I walked over to the back door and let Daisy out in the yard while I started getting ready. I threw on some leggings and an oversized sweatshirt, brushed my teeth, threw my hair up in a top knot, swiped some mascara through my thin lashes, and was ready. I let Daisy back in, grabbed my bag and keys, and was on my way.

"Good morning, Sadie!" my neighbor, Chelsea, called over as I locked my door.

I went over to where she stood, supervising the movers and her husband, Rick.

"Good morning! I didn't know you guys were moving."

"It's been a *very* last-minute thing. My job told me last week that I needed to move to the Iowa office, so here we are. We're not thrilled about it, but it's an opportunity—good or bad, who knows." She looked sad, and I could understand why. As chilly as it was here, at least we had some beautiful foliage. The Midwest seemed flat, dry, and barren.

"I'm sad to see you go but excited for this new opportunity. When is your last day here?"

"Today . . ." Her eyes fell.

"That's so soon! I wish I knew earlier this week, I would've suggested we get dinner, or I could have come over and helped you both pack."

"With all the snow, none of us were outside at all, and I didn't want to come to ring your bell with this news."

I nodded. "I'm going to miss you both—it's been wonderful having you as neighbors."

"You as well, Sadie. I hope whoever moves in here loves it as much as we did. Maybe it'll be a nice, single guy, and you'll fall head over heels for him. That'd be such a cute story!" Chelsea laughed.

"Yeah, that only happens in the books I read, Chels." It was my turn to laugh; she was always one to dream big.

"Hey, stranger things have happened," she said with a wink.

We chatted for a few more minutes before saying our good-byes. Then she headed back inside, and I got in my car, deciding that my first stop for the day was going to be for coffee. The town of Red Oak was so small that you needed to go into the next town over, Leeds, if you wanted coffee or to go shopping. I drove the half hour into Leeds and sat in the coffee shop drive-thru for longer than I wanted, but the sun was out, I had *Midnights* blasting through the speakers, and despite the coolness in the air, it was beautiful.

When the first sip of caffeine hit my lips, it breathed life into my still sluggish body. I didn't think I was used to getting so much sleep and it reminded me of how my mom always said that if you slept more than needed, you would wake up groggy. The woman designed coloring books for a living, I didn't know whether she was the most reliable source for sleep studies, but I also didn't know much on the topic, so who was I to argue with her?

Pulling into the mall, I took inventory of all the stores that I didn't need anything from but knew I would end up stopping in when I was inside. The first, and theoretically the last, stop on my list was the craft store. I had recently picked up crocheting, so I needed some more yarn for the blanket I was making. Sephora caught my eye, and, well, it would have been silly not to go in; I needed a new concealer to hide these horrible dark bags that had been forming under my eyes. The sales associate certainly did her job, and not only did I come out with the concealer, but I also bought a whole new makeup regimen. I parked near Nordstrom, so naturally, when I was done with all the other stores, I had to peruse on my way out. I picked up a pair of brown knee-high boots and a handbag to match, which was perfect for the outfit I was planning on wearing to my mom's birthday in a few weeks.

I'd be the first to admit it; I had a shopping problem, not one that would send me to Shopaholics Anonymous, but one where my debit card should be frozen into a block of ice when I went to the mall. I had a "you only live once, so treat yourself" attitude. I didn't always look at life like this, but after Ben and I broke up and my graphic design business exploded overnight, I realized that I could always make more money, so I made sure to treat myself now and again.

All the unnecessary purchases were loaded up in my car, so now it was time to head to the only other store I *needed* to go to— the grocery store. For this, I had to head back into Red Oak, so I hit play on a new episode of my favorite true crime podcast and drove my happy self the thirty minutes to the store.

I grabbed a shopping cart, pulled my phone out of my bag for my grocery list, and started down the aisles, wandering up and down despite already being out longer than I had planned. Since you never knew when it would snow in Vermont, you were obligated to stock up on all the essentials whenever you were at the grocery store. What did I consider essentials? Dog treats for Daisy (I gave up on making all her treats at home after only two months), milk, bread, snacks, fruit, and vegetables. Somewhat healthy until you added in all the cookies and muffin mix I also tossed in my cart.

When I was in the frozen section by the pizzas, I remembered that I had a new bag in the car, and I wanted to switch it out immediately, so I sped up the last few aisles. With my head in the freezer, I grabbed the last few items on my list when someone bumped my cart. Immediately, I thought, *Okay, who's going to be the one to tell this tourist?* We were a very courteous town and people apologized if they looked at you the wrong way, so a cart bump without one was a rarity around here. I looked up to see who the culprit was. My eyes met one of the most objectively handsome human beings on this planet.

This was a small town, and this guy's face wasn't registering on my radar. I brushed my sandy blonde hair out of my blue eyes and stared at him, my annoyance with his rudeness fading away. I didn't think he noticed my staring from three feet away, which was good because I was *definitely* taking him in. His black hair was on the longer side and his eyes appeared to be the most beautiful shade emerald green. He was bundled up, but I could see from his hands and face that his skin was beautifully sun-kissed—clearly I'd been right, he wasn't from our neck of the woods; we're all pale as can be here. His build remained a mystery since we were in the tundra, and it was thirty degrees out, so he had on an oversized puffy coat.

I cleared my throat, hoping to catch his gaze . . . nothing. I tried again. This time, he glanced at me, irritated, and then back down at the waffles he had in his hands. I was a pretty friendly person; I was even given the Most Friendly senior superlative in high school.

"Excuse me," I called over the two carts between us. I had no idea what I was planning on saying, but here went nothing.

His stare was cold and emotionless, and his tone was flat when he said, "Do I know you?"

"No, I just haven't seen you around here before; I just wanted to welcome you to Red Oak. That's all." I was thrown off. Everyone I encountered was always friendly; this guy was a bit of a prick.

"Oh." He went back to looking at the damn frozen waffles.

"Well, I hope you have a great day," I said, passing by. He stared at me again. Up close, his bright green eyes were icy. Maybe my parents had been right when I was younger, I shouldn't talk to strangers. Even though he was nice to look at, I didn't get a good vibe from him.

I walked away, thrown off by this guy. I brushed it aside, grabbed the remainder of the items I needed, and headed over to the checkout lanes. Once I was all paid and everything was loaded in my SUV, I went back to my house and put it all away. My pantry and refrigerator were stocked once again, and life was good. An hour after I got home, I saw Chelsea and Rick's moving truck drive away, a pang of sadness in my chest. Having the unit next to me open made me anxious—I had lost my security. I immediately went online and ordered a DIY security system for peace of mind.

Their truck hadn't been gone but an hour before the maintenance and cleaning crews were there to do repairs and clean—they must have already lined someone up for the unit and needed a quick turnover. I tried not to be too nosey and went about my business, doing some light cleaning, playing with Daisy, and doing some meal prepping for the week.

I texted Audrey to ask her if she wanted to come over and keep me company. Over the last three years, I'd gotten better with the loneliness, but now and then, it crept back in, and I called Audrey to play blocker. All it ever took was a "what are you doing," and she was at my front door.

Fifteen minutes after sending the message, Audrey was at my house.

"I'm here!" she called from the doorway.

"Come in!" I didn't bother moving from my place on the couch.

"Well, don't you look cozy." She shrugged off her coat and draped it over the coat closet door handle.

"Oh, I am. There's another one over there," I said, pointing to the basket filled with blankets in the corner of the living room.

She grabbed her favorite blue-striped one and plopped down on the couch. "So, what are we watching?"

"*The Bachelorette*, is that okay?" I asked, eyes fixated on the television.

"Yup. Can you pass the popcorn and chocolate?" She reached her hand out expectantly.

"I just ate the last of the popcorn; there's another bag in the pantry." I handed her the empty bowl, and she went to make more. A minute and forty-five seconds later, a buttery scent filled the air.

"Now it smells like a movie theater in here." Audrey laughed, re-taking her seat on the couch, and placing the bowl between us.

The more we watched *The Bachelorette*, the more the water I drank wasn't strong enough. When the show ended, I knew I needed a margarita.

"Snow margarita?" I asked, removing myself from my cocoon of blankets.

"Can you make it a cranberry margarita for me?"

"You've got it." As I was grabbing a small can of cranberry juice, I realized that a cranberry one sounded good, so I grabbed another. I filled the cup with snow, then in a separate glass, I mixed the cranberry juice, lime, and tequila and then poured it over the snow and mixed.

I returned to the couch, drinks in hand. "Your margarita—extra lime juice and sugar around the rim."

"You truly are amazing."

CHAPTER 4

Audrey

WHEN YOUR BEST FRIEND CALLS ON A SATURDAY afternoon, you go running. When Ben broke up with Sadie, she was utterly broken, and over the last three years, I had done my best to be there for her when she was having a rough time, today included. We sat and watched *The Bachelorette* for a while, catching up on the last few episodes. I was in charge of the remote, while Sadie was responsible for keeping the margaritas coming.

When nine-thirty rolled around, we'd had too many to be able to make dinner or drive ourselves anywhere, so we ordered some Chinese food and had it delivered. We turned on a new rom-com and ate our dinner while chugging some water to help keep ourselves hydrated and maybe stave off tomorrow's hangover. We made another round of margaritas when we finished dinner and watched some more television.

I picked up my phone, checking the time. "It's almost midnight!"

"Is it?" Sadie's words were slightly slurred.

"It is. I'll stay here tonight if that works . . . I'm clearly in no shape to drive."

"Of course," she said as a yawn escaped her mouth, "I'll grab you a pillow; there's an extra comforter in the closet in my office."

Sadie went to let Daisy out for the final time of the night, handing me a pillow, and I went into her office and closed the door, getting the sleeper sofa ready. As I placed the comforter on the mattress, I realized I was one of the only people who had slept on this; everyone else lived close enough. Granted, I did as well, but my overnight visits were usually due to alcohol consumption. We were responsible in our old age.

Head spinning, I lay down and closed my eyes, trying to get some sleep. As soon as my head hit the pillow, my mind started to race—a telltale sign I'd been drinking. I kept thinking about work, my failed relationships, my parents' upcoming move, and Sadie. Despite being friends for so many years, I'd always felt like the Robin to her Batman.

I was wide awake until well after two in the morning, mostly because of the car that was sitting nearby with its headlights on. While it was odd, I tried to ignore it, people did weird shit all the time. At some point, I fell into a deep sleep because the next thing I heard was a truck hitting the speedbumps outside the house. I reached for my phone to check the time: it was almost ten. Being nosey, I removed myself from the surprisingly comfortable bed and headed to the window to see what was happening.

I opened the shades and was blinded by the sun, instantly regretting my decision to have so many margaritas last night. There was already a moving truck next door; now *that* was a quick turnaround. *Didn't Sadie's old neighbors just move out yesterday?* I couldn't help thinking. I stood there and waited to see who was moving in when I caught a glimpse of him. My eyebrows shot up, and I felt like my hangover had lifted.

CHAPTER 5

Sadie

I WAS WOKEN UP BY AUDREY'S INCESSANT KNOCKING ON MY bedroom door. "Sadie! Wake up. I have news!"

She was way too chipper for it being this early and for having giant margaritas last night.

"What? Come in," I called from my bed, Daisy still sound asleep at the bottom of the bed.

The door opened. "No, I need you to get up right now and come with me."

"There's nothing worth me getting out of my bed right now, that I can promise you." I pulled the blankets over my head like a petulant child.

"Not even a hot new neighbor?" she asked, eyebrows wagging in delight.

"No, not even that. I don't care that it is . . ." I said as I glanced at the clock on my nightstand, "after ten, I just want to lie here for a while. My head is pounding."

"Please, you won't be disappointed." Audrey's bottom lip jutted out.

I sighed, less than pleased that I was getting up. She knew people watching—handsome men watching especially—was a favorite pastime of mine, but not after margaritas. I joined her, and we walked into my office, peering through the blinds, only seeing the moving men going in and out of the truck.

"Are you sure it was the new tenant, not a mover?"

"I think so; he didn't have that uniform T-shirt on. He's hot as hell: black hair and a killer tan. We should go for a walk with Daisy once we get dressed and can stand the sun once again."

"You mean so we can casually stroll by and see if we conveniently run into him?"

Audrey nodded.

"We can do that," I replied, skeptical of this situation.

We made a quick brunch, changed into clothes we could go outside in, and went out to see this new neighbor under the guise that we were taking Daisy out for a walk . . . not that she minded. If you wanted to go on a walk, you had to spell it out so she didn't lose her mind and start running all over the house.

"Daisy, do you want to go on a wal—" I could barely get the words out before she started to bounce around the entryway, waiting for her leash to be attached to her collar.

We walked down the block and had no luck; he must have been in his house. On our way back, we could see that he was outside chatting with one of the movers, so we sped up a bit. Once we got closer, his face looked familiar, but I couldn't place him. I took a second look—it was the guy from the grocery store. What are the damn odds? I put two and two together and realized he probably wasn't from here, so welcoming him was probably off-putting. As we walked by, I raised my hand and gave a small wave, the look of realization washing over his face—the weird girl from the grocery store was his new neighbor. He looked even more annoyed by my presence.

"He's good-looking but seems ... odd," Audrey whispered in my ear when we walked up to my front door.

"Wait until we get inside," I replied through gritted teeth.

No sooner had I closed and locked the door than Audrey was at it. "What was that guy's problem? Why was he so weird when you waved? He's so unfriendly. That takes his level of attractiveness down from a ten to a solid five."

"So, fun fact, I met him yesterday at the grocery store. He bumped into my cart, so I welcomed him to the town. What a colossal failure. He just looked at me like I was the biggest inconvenience in the world."

"Well, that was rude. Now you're going to have a rude asshole that lives next door."

"I mean, yeah, it was rude ... but honestly, as long as he's quiet and leaves me alone, I don't care who lives next door. I did order a security system, finally."

"Well, I was hoping for some enemies-to-lovers trope, but I guess him just leaving you alone is fine too ..."

I laughed. Audrey was a big fan of seeing enemies become lovers in her romance books, so she must have been thinking three years down the road and not in the present day. "It'll all be good. From our two interactions, I think he will be a quiet guy. Hopefully, he's only here for a few months, and then someone else, perhaps an attractive guy who *is* friendly, will move in, and then he and I can live happily ever after."

"Now that's more like it. Although, I do hold out hope that this may be a grumpy and sunshine situation, and Mr. Grumpypants will fall madly in love with you."

"Don't hold your breath on that one; he doesn't seem like the small-talk type."

"That's what they all say," Audrey added with a wink.

She left soon after we got back from our walk, leaving me alone, once again, with my thoughts. If my new neighbor wanted nothing to do with me, that was fine; I would just keep going about my business and wave hello when I saw him outside.

After dinner last night, we'd had a buzz going from our margaritas, so we just left the plates in the sink. I paid for it now because last night's laziness became a task on today's to-do list. I loaded up the dishwasher, wiped down the counters, and opened my laptop to plan my week. Every Sunday afternoon, I looked at what I need to design in the coming week and what client calls I'd have and then plan accordingly. While last week was busy, this one was going to be even worse.

That was one thing I loved about working for myself; I was able to set my hours and plan around something I had to do; conversely, I also had to have the self-discipline to work the hours I set. I was very fortunate—I started my business when I graduated college six years ago, and it had grown exponentially over the last three years. I took on some big Silicon Valley clients, especially with tech startups that didn't have in-house graphic designers.

As much as being broken up with by the man I thought I would marry ripped my heart to shreds, it also taught me who I was as a person. I had always relied on others, so being tossed out on my own allowed me to grow into who I was today: Sadie Augustine, graphic designer, dog mom, and soup connoisseur.

CHAPTER 6

Sadie

I T WAS SEVEN IN THE MORNING WHEN MY ALARM STARTED beeping loudly, rudely waking me up from my deep sleep and wonderful beach-filled dreams. I turned it off and rolled onto my back, rubbing my eyes and staring at the ceiling before registering that a bunch of noise was coming through the wall. I listened closely, it sounded like a drill or a power tool, but I couldn't make it out. Mr. Grumpypants must have been hanging stuff on the walls inside the master bedroom . . . an ungodly early hour to do so, but whatever.

I got up and decided to take Daisy on a walk instead of just letting her outside because it had started snowing again; I mentally patted myself on the back for stocking up when I went to the grocery store over the weekend. I got changed and glanced at myself before heading out on our walk; I looked like I lived in Antarctica. Actually, that wasn't fair to the people of Antarctica. They probably wore fewer layers than I did during the winter.

Living in Vermont wasn't ideal for someone who was chronically cold, but it was home. My dad always joked that I had no blood because I would always sit on the couch with a blanket on my lap. It didn't matter if it was the middle of the summer and we had the air conditioner on, a blanket was always near.

We walked around the neighborhood and watched the snowfall, the frigid air blowing in my face. Daisy was having the time of her life trying to catch the snowflakes while I was just trying to preserve my freezing, gloved fingers. We took the shortcut because I'd had enough of taking snowflakes to the eyeballs. It was like a halo of light around my front door, welcoming me home. When I opened the door, the heated air enveloped us like a warm hug, but I was still freezing. I took off Daisy's leash and my multiple layers and went straight to the bathroom to take a hot, skin-burning shower to warm up. I turned on some relaxing music and hopped in, taking my time.

When I got out of the shower, the bathroom mirror was fogged up, and my skin was red and splotchy—the hotter the shower, the better, even in summer. I got changed into a nice top with sweatpants for my few client calls this morning. I put on the new makeup I bought on Saturday and went to the kitchen to make a cup of tea. On days when it snowed, I always opted for tea over coffee; there was something about it that suited the weather.

I sat down at my desk and opened my laptop, finally ready to get started for the day. I had two back-to-back client calls, and then the rest of my day was free to actually get some design work done. I was in the zone today, so I didn't look up until some movement outside on the lawn caught my eye. Mr. Grumpypants was hanging up a security camera—he was clearly weary of this area. I took this as my opportunity to go outside to get the mail and try to spark a conversation again. It had been almost a week since he moved in, and I hadn't tried to contact him. I threw on my puffy coat and went to the mailbox at the edge of the front yard.

I waved and called out, "Good afternoon!"

Again, he stared blankly at me, so I continued, "It's me, Sadie, the girl who approached you at the grocery store." I could see it all over his face. He knew exactly who I was and was just playing it off like he didn't.

Finally, he spoke after several seconds of uncomfortable silence. "I'm Liam. I'm new to the area."

He speaks! "I figured. You're way too tan to be from Vermont, we all look like vampires here."

I saw the corner of his mouth perk up the slightest bit. "Yeah, you all are pretty pale."

"We are. Sorry for being so forward the other day at the store . . . I just try to be friendly. Might want to get used to it since everyone here will be more than welcoming."

He still didn't seem to be in the mood for a conversation when he said, "It's all good. I just wasn't expecting it was all."

Maybe Audrey was right. Under this frosty exterior was a kind human being, one who was just shy.

"I understand how that could be off-putting." I looked down at the mail in my hand, "Well, I don't want to interrupt what you're doing, so I guess I'll see you around." I started for the front door and heard a "See you soon" called out behind me.

I smiled inwardly and went back inside, where Daisy greeted me at the door as I hung up my coat, immediately rolling on her back, wanting her furry golden stomach scratched. I happily obliged for a few minutes before heading back to my desk to finish up my work for the day.

I knew how I worked best: I kept normal 9-to-5 hours, stacked my mornings with client calls, stepped away from my desk for lunch, and then did all my design work in the afternoons when my creativity peaked. It worked well, and I made six figures doing this freelancing thing—I found that some more prominent brands preferred to work with smaller designers and ran with it.

I lived a very unassuming life; I didn't want fancy cars or a mansion; I wanted to set myself up well for when I eventually bought some land and built a house.

I started designing a logo for a new clothing boutique opening up on East Main Street; the client wanted something light, flower-filled, and pink. I created a beautiful soft pink floral arrangement and sent it off for approval. Then made some edits to a flier for a pharmaceutical company and sent that off for final approval. I looked up at the clock on my computer screen; it was almost five, so I called it quits for the day.

It had stopped snowing, so Daisy and I went for our afternoon walk around the neighborhood. There was a distinct chill in the air, which you only felt when snow was near. As we approached our house, I felt the first cold prick on my nose—the snow was starting back up. We made it in just in time before it started coming down and watched it fall from our spot by the window.

I had prepped some veggies the other day, so I started to make a chicken soup with wild rice, the most superior soup of them all. I sautéed the chicken breasts, took them out, then added in the onions and garlic, cooking those down a bit until they were nice and caramelized. I added the chicken broth and veggies and brought that to a boil before I added the chicken back in. I seasoned it to perfection and then let it simmer for a while. Once it started to break down, I pulled it out, shredded it, and put it back in. I seasoned it a bit more and then let it cook while I made some rice. I combined the two, added a little bit of grated Parmesan cheese, and it was ready to eat.

I was still thrown off by Mr. Grumpypants—Liam's—behavior. He seemed like maybe he was just shy and not as rude as we had initially thought. I put it out of my mind and flicked on a movie while devouring two bowls of soup. This had the makings of the perfect night—a good film and a delicious dinner. Once the end credits rolled, I reached for the thriller I'd started reading Friday, finishing up the last three chapters before calling Audrey. We were both reading it simultaneously, so naturally, we had to discuss book club style. We spent forty-five minutes talking through the big twist at the end when a yawn escaped my mouth.

"You sound tired, you should head to bed. Didn't you say you had some big deadlines coming up tomorrow?" Audrey asked, also sounding exhausted.

"Yeah, I do have a bunch on tomorrow. I was productive today, but still."

"Why don't you go get some sleep."

"That's my plan. Talk to you later."

"Night," she said.

I let Daisy out for the final time of the night, and once she was back in, we made our way to the bedroom. She plopped down in her dog bed that was next to my side of the bed while I snuggled into the mountain of comforters and blankets that adorned my own. My head hit the pillow, and I was immediately unnerved. I felt like I was being watched. I sat up and turned the lamp on my nightstand on, a shiver running down my spine. I looked around the room and didn't see anything before I looked down at Daisy and saw that she was completely unbothered. If someone was here, Daisy would be up and on high alert, but instead, she was cuddled up in her bed.

Still not feeling settled, I flicked on the television and put on a cooking show, that would distract me from these weird feelings. I attributed it to the book I was reading—the main character was being stalked, I had probably just internalized it.

CHAPTER 7

Liam

MOVING TO VERMONT WAS NEVER ON MY BUCKET LIST. I planned to stay in Florida with my friends and just live the coastal lifestyle—boating to dinner, spending every day at the beach, and living off seafood. Unfortunately, my dad's health was declining, and he needed someone nearby if something were to happen. When my parents split up all those years ago, my dad moved up here to Vermont, and I only saw him for holidays, so we didn't have the best relationship, but when he called, I knew what I needed to do.

I'd found this apartment complex on a whim. I needed someplace somewhat inexpensive and close to my dad—he was only fifteen minutes away, so this was the perfect location. My goal with this move was to keep to myself and blend it, but this Sadie girl next door was making that difficult. She was stunning; I didn't think she understood how beautiful she looked when she was all bundled up and taking her dog for a walk. She wanted to be friendly, but I knew, as sad as it sounded, this was only tempo-rary. I wasn't going to live here forever and, therefore, didn't want to get attached to anyone or anything.

For the last month, I'd kept to myself, doing my best to stay inside and only leave if I had to. If I had to go to the grocery store, I would run out at night to interact with as few people as possible. Sadie must work from home because she didn't leave her house very often—mainly only on weekends. That sounded creepy, but I could hear her garage door open and close. We'd run into each other at our mailboxes a handful of times, but nothing was said, just some small smiles exchanged. I could tell it was killing her; she just wanted to start a conversation, but I had shut her down twice, so she didn't even bother anymore. That's not who I was; back home, I was friends with everyone I interacted with. Even though I was thirty, I was still always the life of the party—bring-ing new people into our group of friends all the time and making them feel at home.

Now that I was settled, maybe I should try to be friendly with Sadie, more than the small half-smiles I'd been giving her. I can only imagine what she'd said about me to her friends. Probably something along the lines of "This guy moved in next door and is so rude. He also never leaves his house."

CHAPTER 8

Sadie

I WOKE UP THIS MORNING BEFORE MY ALARM, A RARITY FOR me. The sun was shining, and Daisy and I went for a walk, taking in the crisp late-April morning air. We did our two laps around the neighborhood before heading back home. As we approached the door, there was something on the welcome mat; it looked like a piece of paper. I brought Daisy inside before grabbing it. "Sadie" was written in neat cursive on the white envelope. This was placed, not mailed—didn't love that.

I brought the envelope inside and looked down at Daisy as I said, "Here's to hoping this isn't a letter from a stalker or contains some sort of Anthrax." I made the joke, but it was a real possibility—who just dropped off a note at someone's doorstep?

I inhaled sharply and opened the envelope, pulling out a small, folded piece of cream paper. My shaking fingers slid over the paper, opening it up.

Sadie –

I wanted to apologize for how rude I've been over the last month. My crankiness is two-fold: I'm moving here from Florida, so I'm not used to the cold, and this move wasn't exactly my idea. I'd love to start over, are you available for dinner tonight? I know this is old-school, but I didn't have your phone number. If you're interested, meet me outside at six. We can grab dinner somewhere.

Hope to see you tonight,
Liam

An involuntary smile spread across my face; I wasn't a wrong judge of character; he was just cranky about being here, which I understood because this cold often made me grumpy, too. I texted Audrey to let her know about these new developments. Nearly every day, Audrey would text me to see if I had talked with Liam; the answer was always no . . . until today.

> Audrey: Didn't I tell you this would be an enemies-to-lovers situation?
>
> Sadie: Technically, yes. But I don't think the handful of small interactions we had would equate to "enemies."
>
> Audrey: Well, whatever! Are you going to go?
>
> Sadie: I'm debating it. I don't know if it's a date or not.
>
> Audrey: Definitely a date. Go. You've not been on one in years.
>
> Sadie: Yeah, dating Ben worked out so well, didn't it? Lol
>
> Audrey: Just because he was an asshole doesn't mean Liam will be! Take the chance; what's the worst that could happen?
>
> Sadie: I guess you're right; I'll go.

I went ahead and started my work for the day. I knew I had a few deadlines that were due today, so on days like this, I try my best not to schedule any client calls to keep my head down and work. I opened the Netflix app on my iPad and picked a home organization show as background noise while I worked. I put my head down and worked until my iPad died a few hours later. Taking this as a sign, it was time for some food. I took a longer lunch break because I was more productive this morning than anticipated. I had a smaller meal since it was already 2:30, and then opted for a shower to get ready for this dinner. I had decided to go—what *was* the worst thing that could happen? We'd go out once, and if it was awkward, then we'd just wave uncomfortably to each other when we were both outside for the foreseeable future. So, really, nothing would have to change.

I already knew that I was going to spend some time getting ready. I wasn't putting all my eggs in one basket, but this was my first date (if that was what we were calling it) in a while, and I wanted to look nice. I put on my favorite jeans and a floral print blouse and gave my body a once-over in the mirror; my outfit made my average frame look slightly slimmer. I brushed my freshly washed hair and let it air dry for a bit, I'd style it later. For now, I was going to get back to work, finish up early, and call it a productive day.

I was able to wrap up my final design and send it off for critiquing by 4:30, giving me the perfect amount of time to properly freak out about what this dinner was. *Was* it a date? Was it just someone trying to be friendly? I knew I was overthinking it, but that was just who I was as a person, an anxious mess most of the time but extremely friendly. I chose to think it was just two neighbors getting to know each other, so that it would take some of the pressure off.

Physically unable to turn my brain off, I reached for the book I had been reading the last few days. With only a handful of chapters remaining, I knew I could throw myself into it, and it would help to calm my nerves. Well, I was wrong. My nerves might have been calm about dinner, but the twist at the end of the book had me wholly shaken up. The ending had you wondering what to even believe. Mind blown. I glanced up at the clock and only had forty-five minutes before I was supposed to meet Liam, so it was time to fix my hair. It took a while, but I straightened it, put some makeup on, and accessorized. I examined myself in the full-length mirror; it had been so long since I'd been on a date that I forgot how nice it felt to get dressed up. As I was leaving the bathroom, I could have sworn I saw something walk by my bedroom window. It had the outline of a person, but I couldn't be sure. Was someone in my backyard? I grabbed the pepper spray sitting on my dresser and walked over to the sliding glass doors, unsure of what I was going to see. Daisy was in my office, so she wouldn't have seen anything. I peered out the doors, seeing the entire yard ... no one was there. I really needed to stop reading such intense thrillers because now apparently I thought everyone was out to get me.

Time flew when you were stressed; did you know that? I let Daisy out in the backyard for a few minutes to do her business and run around, but not without standing by the doors, watching to make sure no one was out there. Standing there, I started internally panicking about this dinner. Before dates, Audrey and I did a massive perusing of the Internet, trying to gather information about the guy—especially likes and dislikes. You only went out with no information on the person once ... trust me, it was awkward. This time, all I had was the first name, so despite my best efforts, my searching was fruitless. I let Daisy back in, put some fresh food and water down for her, and kneeled so I was nose-to-nose with her as she sat patiently. I gave her some scratches on the top of her head. "You don't think this is a bad idea, do you, sweet girl?" I asked, wishing she could talk. Instead, she cocked her head and just looked at me. *So unhelpful.* The clock said 5:58, so I put my shoes and jacket on and headed out the front door, stomach in my throat.

CHAPTER 9

Liam

I KNEW THE WAY I ASKED SADIE OUT WAS SKETCHY, BUT THERE was no other option. I didn't have her phone number, and it felt creepier to knock on her door and ask, which, in hindsight, would have probably been the better option. I wanted to apologize for how rude I have been to her since moving in; it wasn't representative of who I was, and I needed to show her that.

The first order of business was showering and looking like a presentable human being because how I looked right now would make Sadie think that I was a disheveled guy. I hopped in the shower, trimmed my rapidly growing black stubble, then got changed into some black jeans and a blue Henley. I gelled my hair and spritzed some cologne, and I was ready—ten minutes ahead of schedule. It had been five years since I last went on a first date, so I felt very much out of my comfort zone.

I definitely didn't say this was a date, so what if Sadie thought I just want to be her neighbor? Granted, based on looks alone, I would date her, but it was probably best I got to know her a little bit better before I started calling anything a date; that would scare anyone off. I wore a light jacket because I didn't expect the temperature to drop this much at the end of April, and headed outside.

Not knowing if she would even show up weighed heavily on me. I was early, so I stood by my front door, wiping my hands on my thighs every thirty seconds. I was going to walk over to the mailbox to wait, but I heard her door open just then. Success.

I walked across the lawn, the grass crunching under my feet. "Hi, neighbor!"

CHAPTER 10

Sadie

I turned and jumped; Liam was no more than six feet away from me. How did he walk so quietly?

I smiled warmly. "Hi . . . this was certainly unexpected."

"I realized I've been a real jerk, so I wanted to make it up to you. I'm obviously new here and don't know what's around. Do you have any suggestions of where we could go?"

"I appreciate that. I have an early morning, so would you mind if we stayed close?" He seemed like a completely different person now. Maybe being mid-move had been the reason behind his mood.

"That works. I'm starving, so I'll eat anything."

"Why don't we head to East Main Street and get some Delmonico's? It's the best pizza place in town. They have other stuff, too, if you're not in the mood for pizza."

"Pizza sounds fantastic. I've not had a good slice of pizza in a while. I can drive, but I'll need some directions." He smiled, and all the anxiety I had melted away. Maybe this was the start of something good. We walked over to his driveway, and he opened the door of his Audi for me—very chivalrous. The restaurant was barely seven minutes away, so we made small talk about the weather on our way.

We were greeted as soon as we walked through the door by the owner, Dom, and seated at a cozy booth in the corner. I think he could read between the lines and realized we were on a date, so he put us away from others so we could have some privacy, which I appreciated. We were handed our menus, and I looked around, admiring the restaurant I had been in countless times over the course of my life. This restaurant used to be run down, but when Dom inherited some money, he redid the place. The walls were now a pale green, the floors a beautiful white tile, and the once ripped-to-crap booths were refinished with black faux leather.

I had been here enough to know what I wanted and I never varied my order: A small cheese pizza with pepperoni, two garlic knots, and an unsweetened tea. I flipped through the menu once to look like I didn't come here almost every week and get the same thing.

"So, what's good here?" Liam asked, pulling me out of my head.

"Everything, if I'm honest. I definitely would recommend the pizza," I said with a laugh. Obviously, a pizza place had good pizza, Sadie . . .

He laughed, which made me feel better. "That's good to know, I'll just take that suggestion then."

No sooner had he finished his sentence than Dom came over to take our order. "What are you both thinking you want to order this fine evening?" He paused before continuing, looking directly at Liam and saying, "Hold on, this here is a new face in my restaurant, when did you move here?"

"Good evening, sir," Liam said warmly, "I'm Liam Reynolds; I just moved here this week from Florida. I'm Sadie's new neighbor."

Dom looked skeptical, like he knew Liam from somewhere, but seemed to brush it off because that would have been impossible. "Well, it's nice to meet you. Welcome to our quaint town. Now, what can I get you both?"

Liam looked at me, encouraging me to go first, so I spoke up, "Small cheese pizza with pepperoni, two garlic knots."

"Unsweetened tea, as well?"

"You know it!"

"At some point, you *will* get sick of that combination, Sadie bug." A wide smile spread across Dom's face, and his white teeth shined brightly, "And for you, Liam?"

"I'll start with water and a small Caesar salad, then I'll take a medium sausage and pepperoni pizza, please." He was ordering a salad. *He's healthy*, I thought. While ordering his food, I took the opportunity to look at him properly for the first time since our interaction at the grocery store. His black hair touched the top of his ears, his tan, chiseled face stared at Dom with kindness, and now that his coat was off, I could see his muscles underneath his blue Henley. The color of the shirt perfectly complimented his green eyes.

"So, let me break the ice. I know I left you that note this morning to say sorry, but I wanted to do so in person as well." Liam paused, taking a deep breath before adding, "I'm not a guy that likes the cold very much, so moving here wasn't at the top of my to-do list. I moved here to be closer to my father. He left my mother and I years ago, and he's not doing so well, so I decided to move here to take care of him. I miss Florida, I miss being warm, and I miss my friends. It's not an excuse for my behavior, I just wanted to let you know where I was coming from. I hope you can forgive me."

This seemed like a legitimate situation. "It was kind of you to move back here to take care of him . . . I'm sorry to hear that he's not doing well."

He didn't seem like he wanted to talk much about it when he nodded at my statement, so I left it alone. Our drinks came out, and his salad and my garlic knots followed suit. We got to know each other over our appetizers, and discovered we had a lot in common. He, too, was a massive fan of reading, chicken soup with rice, his favorite color was blue, and he seemed genuinely interested in me as more than a neighbor. Fist bump.

Our pizzas came, and we dove on in. After the first bite, I watched as his eyes closed, savoring the taste of the thin, buttery, crunchy crust, the robust tomato sauce, the creamy mozzarella cheese, and the spicy pepperoni and sausage. It's the perfect bite.

"It's good, isn't it?" I asked, enjoying the first bites of my pizza as well.

"This is the best pizza I've ever had. Can I marry Dom so I can learn the recipe?"

A laugh escaped my mouth. "Well, Dom has been happily married for thirty-three years, and I can guarantee you that his wife, Maria, doesn't even know the recipe for any of it. I doubt he will marry some guy off the street and give up his prized possession."

That garnered a chuckle from him. "Okay, that's fair. I guess we just have to come here more often, then." It was a statement but sounded more like a suggestion.

"I try to come here every other Friday—sometimes I eat here, and other times I take it home so I can devour the entire thing and let Daisy have the pizza bones."

"The . . . what?" He was confused, and I didn't blame him.

"Pizza bones, it's what I call the crust. I'm weird and don't eat it, so I give it to my dog as a little treat. Please don't judge." An involuntary smile played on my lips.

"Oh, we used to just call them the pizza scraps. We would

finish a pizza, put some of the crust in the box, put the box on the grass in the backyard, and let our pup out to demolish it all. That was his Saturday night treat. Saturday was pizza night for us."

"I guess all dog owners have some variation of that, don't they?" I asked as we bonded over our love of animals, specifically Golden Retrievers. We sat there for hours while I told him about my friends and job, and he told me about how he was in computer science and worked remotely, giving him the freedom to live anywhere.

Dom periodically checked in on us, topping off our glasses before kindly reminding us at ten that they were closed for the night. Liam paid for my dinner, helped me put my jacket on, and then opened my car door for me—all very gentlemanly things to do—and drove us back to our apartment complex.

We pulled into his driveway, and as I reached for the door handle, he told me to stay put. He got out and again, got the door for me. "That was so unnecessary," I said, flustered.

"It's the least I could do for you."

"You're crazy; you just drove me to and from dinner and paid, you don't owe me anything."

"I wanted you to see that I'm a good guy. I didn't give you a great first impression, so just trying to make up for it is all."

"Well, mission accomplished." We walked over to my front door, the porch light making it look warm and inviting, "Thank you for a nice evening; I had a great time. See you around?"

Liam leaned in, hesitantly pressing a soft kiss to my cheek. "The pleasure was all mine. Are you free to go out for drinks tomorrow night?"

So this *was* a date, and tomorrow would be the second. "Yeah, I think I am. I'd love to get drinks. We can go to a little bottle shop about twenty minutes away, I go there with my friends sometimes and it has a cool atmosphere."

"Perfect, want to meet outside at seven?"

"Works for me." I heard Daisy barking inside; she must have heard us out here. A shiver ran down my spine as I said, "It's a little chilly, I'm gonna head inside. Good night, Liam. Thanks again for a nice time."

"The pleasure was all mine. Stay warm, and I'll see you tomorrow."

I opened the door, and he walked back to his apartment. I turned on the entryway light and Daisy came running over, greeting me with kisses, nearly knocking me over. I shrugged off my jacket, changed into my favorite pajamas, and flicked on the television. I still had adrenaline coursing through my veins. I'd been on a real date for the first time in three years, and he seemed like a lovely guy, one I wanted to get to know even more.

I'd had three relationships in my life. The first was an elementary school relationship, I was in seventh grade, and Mikey Dunham asked to be my boyfriend. Naturally, I said yes, and we "dated" for a month. It made me pretty popular, I wasn't going to lie. The second was with Tyler Williams, and we dated for two years in high school, ending because he moved away for college. My last relationship was with Ben, and we all knew how that ended.

I reached for my phone and texted Audrey, filling her in on the details of my evening. Naturally, she was excited for me. I believed she willed this all into existence—she wanted me to have someone who loved me and could be there at all hours of the day. Could the stranger named Liam next door be the person I'd been waiting for?

I lay down in bed and scrolled on my phone for a bit before my eyelids got heavy. I rolled over and drifted to sleep when I heard a loud bang outside. Jolting awake, I was still for a moment, waiting to hear something else. My heart raced, hoping it was nothing; I couldn't bring myself to look directly at my window. At first, I thought I saw someone walk by, but now I was hearing loud noises. I flicked on the lamp and garnered the courage to turn to face the window. I could have sworn that I saw a dim light out there; maybe it was a flashlight. Regardless, I was now in a state of panic that someone was in my backyard and regretting that I had only installed security cameras in the front of my house.

The smart thing would have been to call the police and have them check it out if I was concerned, but I was sure it was nothing. I didn't hear anything else, and Daisy was still asleep in her bed. I chalked it up to activity in the homes behind our complex. My unit backed up to a row of trees that separated us from some larger ones. Surely both the noise and the light were coming from one of those houses. I wasn't usually awake at three in the morning, so I couldn't be certain if this light was always on or not.

I turned on the television and flipped to *Friends* until I fell back to sleep. Four short episodes later, I heard loud voices coming through the wall—it sounded like Liam was on the phone at . . . I glanced down at my phone, it was five in the morning. I could barely make out his side of the conversation, but could hear his voice was louder than I had heard so far in his month of living next to me.

CHAPTER 11

Sadie

I KNEW I DIDN'T HAVE ANY CLIENT CALLS THIS MORNING AND had gotten all caught up on my design work, and after the night of sleep I had, or lack thereof, I didn't set an alarm. Instead, I let myself have a non-productive day for the first time in forever. Yesterday was a busy one, so today was dedicated to checking emails and organizing my calendar for next month.

February through May were some of my busiest months, so I tried to keep myself as organized as possible. When I rolled over to check the time, I was surprised that it was only eight-thirty, I hadn't slept for nearly as long as I had thought, which was good so I could have the whole day to relax before drinks tonight. I wanted to text Liam to check and see if we were still good for tonight, but I realized I never got his phone number. We'd gotten lost in our conversation, and we must have forgotten to exchange phone numbers, but if anything came up, he could just knock on my door.

I was still full from eating an entire pizza for dinner, so I let

Daisy out, made myself a cup of tea, and we made our way to the couch with my laptop so I could be both lazy and productive. I always sat on the left side of the sofa while Daisy curled up in a ball of fluff on the right side by the back door. It didn't take long, but I got my inbox down to zero and closed my laptop, focusing my full attention on Daisy. "It's not weird that he didn't give me his number, right?" Again, a time I wished she could talk.

Instead of driving myself even more crazy, I clicked the Instagram icon on my phone and typed in "liamreynolds" in the search bar, figuring that might be a safe bet; most people used their first and last names as their usernames. No luck. This time I tried "Liam Reynolds," and a bunch of results came up. I parsed through them, finally finding a picture that looked like him—it looked like a professional photographer had taken it. I clicked the profile, @ LiamR0986, and was sorely disappointed to find that there were only a handful of pictures on the account: a dog watching a sunset, a random selfie, and three photos of the ocean. Nothing out of the ordinary, he probably wasn't a social media kind of guy—the majority of the guys I'd remotely considered dating didn't have a substantial online presence; they were at the point in life where their careers were more important than updating the masses on their whereabouts or what they're drinking. I screenshotted his profile and sent it to Audrey for further inspection. My phone rang immediately.

"You found him!" Audrey paused, inevitably taking a closer look at the screenshot. "Wait, hold on. How closely did you look at his profile?"

"I mean, I looked at the pictures and then sent it over to you, why?"

"He just started posting on this account a month ago . . . to the day . . ."

"And . . .?"

"Nothing, it's just weird."

I got oddly defensive and said, "Maybe he had to create a new profile because his other one was hacked. Maybe he just didn't see the appeal of sharing things online. Maybe, maybe, maybe."

"Yeah, you're probably right. I've seen that lately as well, he was probably a victim as well."

"Exactly, so please let me be happy for once. I enjoyed spending time with him last night." My words had a bit more bite to them than I intended.

"You're right, I'm sorry. Just being protective. Did you get any details on why he moved here?"

"He said his estranged dad isn't doing well, so he moved nearby to take care of him. I forgot to ask where his dad lived, I wonder if we know him."

"His last name is Reynolds?" Audrey asked, clearly having already started a Google search.

"I mean, maybe? Not sure what his first name is, though."

"There is no 'Reynolds' in Red Oak."

"He could live out of city limits, or he could've taken his mom's last name." I laughed. She was getting worked up over nothing. "When we go out for drinks tonight, I'll ask him where he lives and get some more information."

"Yeah, that's true. You're right, I'm sorry."

"It's what friends do . . . you know I'd do the same thing for you."

We chatted a little bit more, and I ended the call, promising to tell her how tonight's drinks date went. My stomach started grumbling around three and I knew if I had a heartier late lunch, then I could handle my alcohol better, so I made myself a ham and cheese sandwich and went back to the couch to resume the movie I was watching. I, unlike Liam, was on social media too much—I scrolled for so many hours today that I completely lost track of time. It was already six, so I had an hour to get ready to go out. I took a quick shower, threw on jeans and a pink paisley print top, and swiped some mascara on my eyelashes and brow pencil over my light eyebrows. I was ready just in time, so I put on my heels and locked up behind me. I looked down at my phone; it was just seven, and he would be out here soon.

I waited five minutes, but no sight of him. Maybe he lost track of time as I did, or perhaps he had a work call that ran over or something. I'd been so far removed from corporate America for so long that I didn't even know if people took calls at seven in the evening. I shifted my purse to my shoulder and walked across the grass to Liam's front door. It looked like he had replaced his doorbell with a smart one, so he could see that it was me and not some random solicitor walking around. Even though he dropped me off in the driveway last night, he must have moved his car to the garage.

I rang the bell and waited.

Thirty seconds.

A minute.

Two minutes.

Three minutes.

The temperature dropped quickly, so I went back inside to wait, greeted by an extremely confused Daisy. Maybe I misheard him and he said 7:30. I sat down on the sofa in my office and turned on the table lamp—my thought was that when he walked over, I would see him and be able to go back outside. Not sure how long it would be, I grabbed a magazine and flipped through it, not paying any real attention. I looked up at every car light that drove by my house wondering if everything was okay with his dad, maybe he had to leave suddenly to take care of him, and since he didn't have my phone number, he couldn't get in contact with me. My mind raced with possibilities, not allowing myself to think that I was being stood up. I didn't want to deal with that hurt.

I looked at my phone again. It was nearing eight-thirty, and my hopes were long dashed. My shoes had long been removed and

I sat there in a fog, saddened because I'd let myself feel like I was worthy of dating again. It had taken me three years to go out on a date. When Ben broke up with me, he ripped out my heart, threw it on the ground, and then drove a semi-truck over it. How did you go from going on beautiful vacations together and enjoying each other's company one day to breaking up out of the blue and giving the other person two days to move their shit out of the house?

If Ben hadn't broken up with me, my business wouldn't have grown like it did, but damn, he was the sole reason for my trust issues. The day he walked out that door after telling me I needed to leave was the last time I had seen him. I deleted him on all my social media accounts, not wanting to subject myself to seeing all his "happily ever after" posts with whomever he was dating. When I finally allowed myself to check earlier this year, he was single and living in California. He always wanted to move out there, so good for him. Enough time had passed that I wasn't angry with him anymore; I had grown to learn that he was merely a supporting character in my book of life. I debated reaching out to him to see how he was doing but knew that would just end poorly for me, bringing back up all those bad memories I had tried so hard to block out.

I flashed back to my current state, on the sofa in my office, being stood up. Tears pricked at the corners of my eyes, one drop threatened to fall. I wouldn't let them, not this time. I was stronger than I was three years ago. I'm not going to let this random guy that moved in next door be the reason why I fell into another dating slump. It was his loss, not mine. I reached for my phone, not sure if I wanted to reach out to Audrey, but decided against it because I didn't want to deal with her probing questions right now. Instead, I called my grandma and asked if she was home. When she said yes, I jumped at the opportunity to go over. I changed into a sweatshirt and was pulling out of the driveway.

No sooner was I out of my car, than the front porch light

flicked on and the front door opened. If she knew you were on your way, my grandma would wait by the window to see when you pulled up and would be at the door waiting. She pushed the storm door open and welcomed me in as I climbed the stairs. No words were exchanged, but I was embraced in a love that I never fully understood the depth and breadth of. There was nothing better than a hug from your grandma. We always had a very special bond that I'd only come to appreciate as I got older.

I kicked off my shoes by the front door and we made our way to the kitchen table. I wasn't sure why, but that was where we always sat and talked. I pulled out the light oak chair, *Jeopardy* blaring on the television. I grabbed the remote and lowered the volume—she refused to wear her hearing aid, so the volume was always eardrum-splittingly loud. Her house always felt like home , cozy ranch-style set back off the main road amongst the trees. When she and my grandpa decorated for Christmas, they would go all out, which drew in people from all over the state.

"Why are you upset?" She might be older, but she was still as sharp as a tack and could see through my bullshit.

"Who said that I was?" I played it off for as long as possible. Whether she even remotely believed me, I had no idea.

"It's not exactly early in the day and you have makeup on. I might be old, but it looks like you had plans of some sort, and they fell through. How close am I?"

There was no avoiding this conversation. "Spot on."

"That's what I thought. Were your plans with Audrey?"

"No, they weren't." I didn't want to admit how stupid I was being over a guy I had barely known for a month.

"With a boy?" Her eyebrows shot up and her eyes went wide.

"Yeah. It's a weird situation."

She went to the refrigerator and pulled out a container of chocolate ice cream, our favorite. Two large scoops went into each bowl before one was placed in front of me.

"Eat up. Then you can tell me about it."

We sat in silence for a few minutes, watching *Jeopardy* (at a normal volume) while enjoying our dessert. The urge to tell her how I felt with each bite grew stronger. Damn her for knowing how to get me to talk.

"So I met him about a month ago . . ."

"There we go," she interrupted, shoving a large spoon of ice cream in her mouth, "Continue."

She always had been bossy. "His name is Liam and I met him at the grocery store. We were in the frozen food aisle and he bumped my cart, so I welcomed him to Red Oak. He looked like he wanted to kill me on the spot for talking to him. It was weird but I didn't care until he moved in next door. He's from Florida, but his dad lives nearby and isn't doing well, so he's taking care of him. We talked more once he moved in, and he's nice, just shy. He left me a sweet note asking me out yesterday, and we went to dinner last night. It went well—or so I thought—so we set a date for tonight to get drinks. I waited for him outside, and he never showed up; I tried ringing the bell and waited there for a few minutes before I went back inside. I waited until I called you. That gets us to right now." I rattled that off quickly.

She paused for a moment. "I see."

"I ramble on, and you say 'I see'?"

"Do you have any strong feelings for him?"

"Not at the moment. I mean, he was really nice and we had a great time, but I wasn't sitting at home planning our wedding today."

That garnered a chuckle out of her. "Then why do you feel this way?"

"I don't know. I'm apparently just a poor judge of character." Why did I have to pick the one person not from here to let some of my guard down? I was stupid and thought he liked me. He just felt bad that he was an asshole and had to make it up to me, so he bought me dinner.

"For starters, you're not a poor judge of character. You were attracted to someone and acted on it. That's quite the improvement from where you were a few years ago, heck, a few months ago. You wouldn't even entertain the thought of dating, and here you are, making the moves—that's great progress. If he wants to stand you up for your date, then that's his loss; he should respect your precious time. You're a beautiful young woman, don't waste the precious hours you've been given on things that don't bring you joy, won't bring you alcohol, or won't make you money."

I was at a loss for words. She'd never spoken that frankly before. "Going to need clarification on that middle one, grandma."

"The first is if it doesn't make you happy, don't do it. The third is if it doesn't make you money, don't do it. And the second one is not to date a guy if he won't bring you a drink. I didn't waste my time on any boys that weren't willing to order and bring me a frilly drink from the bar."

I rolled my eyes, this woman was crazy. Two of the three pieces of advice were sound, the other, not so much. Who based the person they married on whether or not they were willing to bring them a freaking drink? Apparently, my grandma.

"I'm just saying he doesn't respect your time, so pay him no mind. You have better things to focus on—like this game of checkers we're about to play." She whipped out the checkerboard we always played on, a Disney princess one. She bought it for me when I was six, and even though the box had been taped more times than we'd admit and the board was cracked in half, it had over twenty years of memories; we would never throw it away.

I won the first game. Not sure if it was fair, but she won the second game. It was the first time in history that she allowed herself to win.

"Oh dang it," she muttered under her breath, "that wasn't supposed to happen."

"What wasn't?"

"I wasn't supposed to win." She laughed. "How are you feeling? Any better?"

I sighed; I was better. Something was soothing about her and her house. Maybe it was the warm, woodsy smell. Perhaps it was the plastic-covered couches (that you were barely allowed to sit on). Maybe it was the bowls of ice cream or the Sundays where you could smell the marinara sauce she was making wafting outside the house. Or, maybe it was the countless memories of everyone sitting down for Christmas Eve dinner where there was more food than you knew what to do with.

"Still feeling a little bummed, but being here with you helped. And, you're right, he didn't value my time at all, I could've been doing something else."

"Exactly. Don't let him, or anyone else for that matter, dull the sparkle in your pretty blue eyes. As much as I don't want you to go, it's late, and I'm already anxious about you driving home." She handed me a container of her marinara pasta sauce as a parting gift and hugged me tightly. "Get home safe."

A typical Grandma thing to say. I reassured her that I would be careful and promised to send her a text when I got home, letting her know that I had made it safely. I walked to my car, feeling better than I did when I walked through those doors. I'm not sure what I needed to hear, but whatever it was, it worked; maybe I just needed a hug. Before I even got out of the car, I shot my grandma a text, telling her I was home. She could rest easy tonight.

As I was getting out of the car, a light caught my eye—there was a light on in Liam's front bedroom. I looked for a second before I made my way to my front door, the blinds were cracked just a little bit, enough to see the light and nothing else. I glanced down to grab my front door key, and in the millisecond it took me to look back up, the light was off. Now *that* felt like avoidance. He could have just said he didn't want to go out again; he didn't have to make plans and then bail. What an ass.

I settled in for the night and let Daisy out one last time, poured myself a glass of my favorite Apothic Red, and plopped myself on the couch to catch up on some of my cooking shows while crocheting a blanket. It might have sounded like a boring night to many, but I don't care because it chilled me out. I was thoroughly engrossed into my second episode of *MasterChef* when I heard weird noises that sounded like a banging in Liam's house. I paused the show and sat for a second, listening for the sound. It happened again, except louder this time. I made my way to my bedroom, putting my ear on the wall. It sounded like he was hanging something on a wall in his apartment. I returned to my show because nobody had time for men and their shit. I knew my worth and that was that.

On my way back to the couch, I went to the sliding doors to close the blinds that led to my backyard. I looked quickly and thought I saw someone peering over the back of the fence. My heart rate sped up, and I shut the blinds and jumped on the couch. I flicked the lamp back on and sipped the wine, debating whether I had actually seen someone or if my eyes were just playing a cruel trick on me. I really needed to get myself in check. The fact that I kept thinking that I was seeing and hearing things at night wasn't sustainable. I wasn't even this on edge when I first moved in here.

I checked the security app on my phone to see if there was anyone in the front of the house. I scrolled through the last hour of footage, not seeing anything concerning. There was a car parked outside, but that was it. Until about five minutes ago when the security footage cut out for a minute around the time when I closed the blinds. The footage came right back up, but now the car was gone. Was I going crazy or was there really someone outside staring in my window?

CHAPTER 12

Sadie

I DIDN'T HAVE TO OPEN MY EYES TO KNOW THAT TODAY WAS dreary. I heard the rain beating on my window and opened one eye, debating how much I needed to work or if I could answer emails in bed all day. My office was cozy, but my bedroom was next-level. While you'd think dark colors would make a room cozy, you'd be surprised to know that white bedding was the move. Since the walls in my house were a pale gray, I hung up removable wallpaper in the prettiest white and navy blue floral pattern on the wall behind my bed. I had dark gray wood furniture, which made it feel nice and warm. The bedding was all white; the duvet was the fluffiest one I could find. All of that made up the perfect room for me. I rolled over onto my back, phone in hand. The best thing about being your own boss was that I made the rules, and I dictated when I worked and when I didn't.

Yesterday was a lazy day, and I knew today was leaning that way too, so it took me a while to muster enough energy to get up and make my way to my office to grab my laptop. I put my computer on the end table and went to the kitchen to make myself a latte. When you lived in a small town subject to extreme weather, you learned to make all your specialty coffees at home. We had *some* coffee shops, but they only knew how to make two things: hot coffee and iced coffee. Fancy, right? Hence my investment in a Nespresso machine late last year. Since then, I'd perfected a hot and an iced caramel macchiato. I mean, everything else was smooth sailing once you perfected your coffee, in my opinion. When my hot macchiato was ready, I grabbed a blanket and the remote for the electric fireplace. I situated myself in a blanket burrito, flicked the television on to HGTV, and reclined on the couch. I didn't care that it was almost May; I still loved to be snug.

Between the possible peeping Tom and the wine last night, I ended up sitting on the sofa sobbing while clutching my blanket because the guy who won *MasterChef* was my favorite and I was simultaneously terrified of whatever was going on outside. I had no intention of opening my laptop before ten; I was going to give myself two hours to enjoy my coffee, read a little, and watch *Fixer-Upper*. Even though I had just pumped myself full of caffeine and should've been bouncing off the walls, my eyelids got heavy, and I could feel myself drifting off to sleep.

It felt like only a few minutes before a loud bang startled me awake. It was similar to the one I heard in the middle of the night the other day. I could feel my heart racing; I looked around and everything was still in place, so I shook it off as thunder. I checked the time; it wasn't even ten yet—I hadn't been asleep for very long. Since I was definitely awake now, I guess it was a good time to start my work for the day. I sorted through emails a bit, making some minor updates to a logo and sending that back over for final review. Subconsciously, I was still listening for another noise. The logical part of my brain knew that it wasn't thunder, but I couldn't think of what else it could have been. Maybe it was something in Liam's apartment and the part of my brain that was protecting itself attributed it to thunder since we were having such a bad storm. I vowed to myself that if I heard it again, I would walk over and see if he was okay.

With the coffee now coursing through my veins and doing what it was supposed to, I dove into some new designs. One of my calls the other morning was with a guy who was starting his own floral arrangement company, and he needed a branding package—logo, letterhead, and website mock-up—so I got to work on that. He was adamant about wanting to stick with some bright colors and incorporating an abstract bouquet. Some graphic designers didn't like working with people who knew exactly what they wanted because it took the creative freedom out of it, but I loved it. I enjoyed seeing people have a vision for their companies, and it was even better when I could bring that to life. There was no better call to receive than "We love this. No edits need to be made!" I was so in my world that when I heard another loud noise, it scared me half to death. My hands were shaking, and my heart hammered in my chest. *That's it.* Pushing my laptop to the side, I was going to get changed and walk over to Liam's because, if nothing else, the noises needed to stop, not only for my sake but for Daisy's. Being a rescue, loud noises scared her.

I went to my closet and put on sweatpants and a sweatshirt, not bothering to brush my hair. I paused for a moment, putting my ear up to the wall in my bedroom to confirm he was home and I wasn't losing my mind. This guy had made it clear last night that he didn't want anything to do with me anymore, but I knew if something had happened to him and he was dead in there, I would like to know before the decomposition smell started to permeate through the walls and into my apartment. I shrugged on my coat and boots, not even bothering to lock my door . . . this wouldn't take long. I was out the door, ready for confrontation. I wasn't making any promises that my feelings about last night wouldn't get in the way. With the cold rain pummeling my face and the cool air pricking my fingertips, I took a deep breath and rang the doorbell. I waited a full minute, knowing damn well he was home. I rang it again and waited. Then once more. He was just in full avoidance mode, and I had learned my lesson. The anger bubbled up inside me, and my fists balled instinctively.

"Liam, I know you're home. I don't care if you don't want to see me; just stop making so much damn noise," I yelled at his door, hoping he could hear me, knowing deep down that it was pointless.

I made my way back across the front lawn and back into my safe space. Daisy must've heard me outside because when I came back in, she didn't even lift her head off her bed. I cozied back up on my couch and resumed my show—I hadn't even turned off the television. I made it through the rest of the *Fixer-Upper* episode before the anger with Liam bubbled back up. My phone was on the couch cushion next to me, a text from Audrey asking about last night sitting unread. Instead of texting everything out, I called her, knowing that the tech start-up she worked at had given all the employees a mental health day and she didn't have plans.

"You ignored my text." No, hi, hello, nothing. Audrey was "mad" that I didn't answer her in a timely enough manner. She was always the first I called when I had a problem or need advice and was always up-to-date with dates and potential boyfriends. I guessed that was part of growing up together and being life-long friends: you felt entitled to every detail of the other person's life. I was guilty of it, too.

"Not intentionally . . ." That was a total lie.

"You're lying." She was good.

There was no point in lying to her. "I had a shit night and took a nap this morning."

"Details. Now. Never mind, I'm coming over. Have a latte ready for me, be there in ten!"

I didn't even have time to respond before she'd already hung up on me. Knowing it was a pointless fight and I had approximately seven minutes before she would walk through my door, I made her the damn latte and myself another macchiato while I was at it. I finished my drink when I heard the front door lock turn. Audrey had a key, because when your best friend listened to as many true crime podcasts as mine did, they demanded to have a key to your house, so if you stopped responding to messages, they could come in and check on you.

"It's me!" Audrey called out from the entryway.

"Your latte is ready, your Majesty."

"You can take your snark elsewhere, Sadie." Audrey laughed as I handed her the latte. Her dark black curls framed her slender, ebony face; I'd always been envious of her. She looked like a supermodel, while I was here looking like Buddy the Elf.

We made our way to the couch, Daisy settling on Audrey's feet.

"Are you ready to hear about my night?" I asked, prepared to acknowledge that I was stood up.

"Spill. I thought it had gone well, and that's why you hadn't texted back."

"Not even close. I went outside at exactly seven and waited for a bit before I rang the bell. No answer. I went back inside and sat for a while, hoping he would show up. Nothing. So, I called my grandma and went over there for a few hours. It helped, but I still feel stupid. I finally go on a freaking date, and I get stood up."

"What a jerk." Her brows furrowed, and she placed her cup on the table, making her way over to my side of the couch to pull me into a hug. She always had this innate ability to give the best hugs. I hadn't even realized a tear escaped, so I brushed it away, hoping she would pretend not to have noticed.

"He's not worth it." I could see the anger in her eyes. "Worst case scenario? You have some awkward encounters with him outside; that's about it."

"I guess, but he was home."

"You're sure about that?" she questioned, eyebrow raised.

"Yeah, I heard some noise last night in what would be his bedroom, I'd assume."

"Huh."

"What?" She was losing me.

"I guess I've never seen this type of situation before where this happens when you're neighbors. I would've thought that if you wanted to stand someone up when you live next door to them, you would leave your house. I mean, that's just how *I* would stand someone up."

"That's a fair point. I hadn't thought of that . . ." Now my mind started to drift.

"Don't spiral; I'm sure it's just me being me."

"There's more . . ."

"Oh great."

I recounted what happened when I got back from my grandmother's then, sparing no detail.

Audrey looked as suspicious as I had felt at the moment. "Interesting. Probably just a . . . coincidence." I knew she didn't believe a word of what she was saying.

"Or maybe there's more."

"Really, Sadie?"

"Last night I thought I saw someone looking over the fence and when I checked the security cameras, there was a car parked there. About the time I closed the blinds, the footage cut out and then when it came back up, the car was gone."

Audrey's eyes got wide, her brows furrowed. "Did you call the police? Please tell me that you called the police!" Her voice was dripping with disappointment.

I couldn't make eye contact with her. In hindsight, I probably should've called the police at least to report it. "I didn't. I'd had two glasses of wine, I couldn't be sure of what I saw. And the car thing could have been a pure coincidence."

I was just trying to make myself believe it at this point.

"Sadie . . ." Audrey shook her head before continuing, "Do you really think it was a coincidence?"

"I don't know. Maybe? It could have been a tree or something. I didn't look this morning to see if anything was there."

"Then maybe it was a good thing you didn't call. I know this isn't the first time you thought you saw something. Maybe you should get some more sleep or something."

I nodded, she was right, I had been working some later nights to meet deadlines, so my sleep schedule was off, plus I hadn't been eating regularly, and my annoyance with Liam left me in a constant state of it.

"So there might be just a little bit more . . ." I held a pillow tight to my chest.

"Sadie!" A vein popped out of her forehead.

I spilled what happened this morning.

"Have you lost your mind?" Her voice was raised, startling Daisy. "It could've been a gunshot; why in the hell did you go over?"

Oh, she was not happy with my life decisions. "I figured something just fell! I wanted to just talk with him and tell him to be quieter."

"You could've gotten hurt; I can't believe you made such a reckless decision. You don't usually do stuff like that." I was being scolded like a child, but honestly, after she said that and I thought about it, it really *was* a dumb move on my part.

"You're right, it was stupid to go over there."

"Just be careful; you don't know this guy at all. I've seen some red flags, but it's not my place to say anything."

"You're my best friend, you can tell me."

Audrey inhaled deeply before she said, "So, I did more research after you sent me his Instagram profile and I couldn't find a thing. I looked in all of the public databases to see if I could find a Liam Reynolds in Florida and couldn't find any."

I opened my mouth to say something and was shushed.

"Let me finish. Since I knew you were going to question it—there was no Liam Reynolds with his physical characteristics in their twenties or thirties in the entire state of Florida. Don't you find it just a little odd that I can't find any record of him in either Florida or here? That we've never heard of his dad in this small-ass town? That his Instagram account was brand new? That he was super weird and then all of a sudden was asking you out? I'm sorry I'm overstepping, but those are some red flags if you ask me."

I let what she said sink in. She was right, and I knew that, but now I was invested from a different angle: figuring out who this guy was. My voice dropped to a whisper, "What if this guy is in the Witness Security Program or something? What if that's why his name is different, and he has a suspicious reason for moving here."

Audrey's eyes lit up. "You're right! Oh, this is fun. It's like a real-life true crime podcast. If he is under witness protection, I wonder why. We should look into this. Are you doing any real work today, or can I stay and we can research?" It wasn't a question but more of a statement.

"I'm not sure if that's a good idea. What if it sets off some government alert or something we're looking into? I feel like we'd be invading his privacy."

"Sadie, what mental gymnastics did you have to do to get to a government alert? Maybe you were right, and he's just low-key, but from my perspective, a weird guy is living next door, and you need to know who he is."

"That's true, but I also don't know anything about any of my other neighbors." I knew that would stump her. Truthfully, I didn't want to even acknowledge Liam's existence. I had one good date and then was stood up; he was dead to me.

"Whatever you say. I'm going to keep researching with what

little information I have, so would you please turn on a movie that would be good for background noise?"

Audrey always made herself right at home here, which I loved. It got lonely in the days just before spring. The world was threatening to bloom, but wasn't quite there yet. There was more rain than usual and the days just felt long and gray. So, it was a welcomed visit when your best friend showed up and was willing to hang out with you for the entire day. I turned on a newly released comedy; I scrolled on my phone on one side of the couch, and Audrey, who clearly came prepared to stay here all day, was on her laptop on the other side.

We sat there, half watching the movie, half in our own bubbles, occasionally talking about the movie. Audrey was typing away furiously on a search engine; I knew better than to ask questions while she was that intense. I zoned out for a few minutes, thinking about the red flags Audrey brought up. While they could easily be a simple misunderstanding, I had to acknowledge that it *was* a little bit strange. When she found him, there would inevitably be a simple explanation and we would both feel silly.

As the movie ended, I heard her typing stop.

"What were you furiously typing away about?"

She jumped. Clearly she was in her own little world. "Gathering my notes."

"On . . .?"

"Your neighbor. I'm not going to call him Liam because I doubt that's even his name." She closed her laptop dramatically, sighing, and putting her head back on the couch, eyes closed.

"Sharing is caring."

She opened her eyes and I could see the concern in her eyes. "I tried searching all avenues but haven't come up with anything. You know that doesn't sit well with me, so I'll keep looking."

"I can see how much this is bothering you, please don't stress about it. I guarantee you it's nothing. I'm just fine over here in my little bubble. How about this? To prove to you that he has a real identity, I'll try to get in contact with him—I'll follow him on Instagram and see what happens. How does that sound?"

Audrey was thinking about it. "Fine," she said eventually, "I suppose that's the best course of action right now. Let's see if we can learn anything else about him for me to look into."

"Deal. On another note, are you staying for dinner or no?" I glanced at the clock and realized it was almost time for dinner, we had skipped lunch.

"Nope, I'm going over to my parent's house. Did you want to come?"

I thought about it . . . it was a free meal and her family always welcomed me with open arms when I showed up unannounced, but still. "I'm good, thank you. Assuming this is your cue to leave?"

It was Audrey's turn to look at the time on her phone. "Yeah, probably. I have to help my mom get some stuff packed up before their move in a few weeks."

"I can't believe they're moving. I feel like that's my house, too, after all these years."

"I'm sad that they're leaving, but I know moving into this smaller house is their dream, so who am I to stop them? It'll be good for them!" Audrey packed up her laptop, said her goodbyes to Daisy and I, and was on her way.

I looked in my refrigerator, hoping for some dinner inspiration. My eyes landed on the jar of marinara sauce my grandma gave me last night and my meal was decided for me: pasta. I made some spaghetti and tossed it with the sauce and topped it with grated parmesan cheese until my stomach grumbled in excitement. I sat on the couch and was enjoying my dinner when I realized I said I would follow Liam on Instagram. I went to my recent searches and clicked on his profile. I looked at each photo again, examining them a little bit closer this time; there were no captions and the only 'likes' on them were from some spam accounts, none of them looking like they were actual people. I looked at the list of accounts he was following, and there were only nine—a meteorologist in Texas, a bookstore down the street, a girl named Hailey, a true crime podcast, three restaurants in Delaware, a Vermont locals account, and McDonald's. What a weird combination of pages. I clicked on the Hailey girl's profile and it looks like she hadn't posted in a few weeks. She didn't have a last name or location on her account, so it was a dead end. I finally worked up the nerve to click the follow button on Liam's profile and immediately closed out of the app. Only time would tell what would happen.

CHAPTER 13

Sadie

FOR IT BEING A FRIDAY, I WAS AWFULLY UNMOTIVATED. I knew that another rainy day was in store for me, but since I didn't do any work yesterday, I needed to double down today. I turned off my alarm and immediately got up and dressed, and by that I in no way meant jeans, but I threw on my favorite leggings and sweatshirt to make the day more bearable. I let Daisy out in the yard and made myself a cup of tea; when that was ready, Daisy had enough of the cold and rain and wanted to come in. We made our way down the hallway into my office and I took a seat at my desk and draped a blanket over my legs while Daisy curled up in her bed on the floor. I put my phone on do not disturb and opened my laptop, ready to start on my work.

I put a podcast on and the morning flew by. I took a break for lunch and checked my phone to find I had one missed call from my mom, a text from Audrey, an email from Barnes and Noble letting me know my pre-ordered book had shipped, and a new Instagram follower . . . @LiamR0986. My heart sped up. I checked when the notification was from—three hours ago. Taking every ounce of my courage, I clicked the Message button and started typing.

> Sadie: Hi, Liam. I know we were supposed to meet up last night and you didn't show, I hope you're okay. You never gave me your phone number, so I had to message you here. Let me know if you need anything.

I only somewhat cared because, at this point, I was genuinely curious and would do what I could to help Audrey figure out what this guy's deal was. There was a ninety-nine percent chance that there was a reasonable explanation for all of this, but it was the one percent that thrilled me. If nothing else, I'd learn a little bit more about my neighbor in the process.

I closed the app and waited for a response. Ten minutes passed before I heard my phone vibrate. A new Instagram message.

> Liam: Hey, Sadie. I'm sorry about last night, I didn't mean to stand you up. I was getting my apartment set up, had headphones in, and lost track of time. I didn't realize what time it was until it was too late. I didn't have your number, so I couldn't let you know what happened. I heard you come home, but it was late and I didn't want to startle you if I knocked on your door. I'd love another chance if you're willing.

That seemed all too plausible. I heard him over there last night when I got home and it did sound like he was hanging things up. That would also explain why I saw the lights on and then I didn't. He wasn't avoiding me, he'd just lost track of time. See, there was the 99% I was talking about. I texted Audrey to let her know that he was just absent-minded, not living under an alias. She responded with an eye-roll emoji, so I figured she would drop it now. I messaged Liam back.

> Sadie: I thought you were trying to avoid me after standing me up. I stopped by this morning because I could hear you doing stuff over there. Assuming you probably had your headphones in. I'd still like to get drinks when you're available.

I felt some butterflies in my stomach; I knew that he should've made an effort to try and contact me yesterday, but he probably felt like he ruined his chance. I really did enjoy spending time with him, he was funny and extremely nice to look at, so I could give him another shot, and see if he showed up. If he stood me up this time, then I'd be left to believe that he was, in fact, a psychopath.

> Liam: I saw that on my doorbell camera a few minutes ago, but yeah, I had my headphones in. Sorry about the noise, I'll try to keep it down. I'm free tonight if you want to get those drinks.

I paused before I replied. I didn't want to come across like I was waiting patiently for his responses . . . even though I was. I put my dishes in the dishwasher and made my way back to my office, trying to think of what to say. Did I even really want to go out with him again? Was he telling the truth? I guess there was only one way to find out, I was going to play hard to get.

> Sadie: As long as I can get caught up on my work, I should be free this evening. What time were you thinking?

Before I even closed out of the message, he had already seen it and was typing. Me being who I was, I immediately exited the thread. I need time to concoct a response before I actually opened the message. I was an overthinker.

> Liam: I don't have headphones in right now, so I should be good to meet at 7 lol. Does that work for you if you're able to get everything done?

Now I needed to decide what I wanted to do. There were three paths that I could take: the first was to tell him yes and stand him up, the second was to just tell him no now, and the third was to say yes and go out . . . if he didn't stand me up again. I couldn't consult Audrey because she would straight up tell me to not go, so I was left to my own devices. I needed to make my mind up quickly. In a split second decision, I typed my response.

> Sadie: Yeah, that should work just fine . . . unless you stand me up again

Did that seem a little aggressive? Yeah, but it was deserved. I could've added an LOL in there to lessen the blow, but I wanted him to know I was frustrated.

> Liam: I promise I'll be outside waiting for you before 7! You have my word.

After reading that message, I liked it, and knew I was going to give him the benefit of the doubt. Stuff like that happened all the time, he *seemed* apologetic, so I'd give him a fair chance tonight. If he blew it, then that was his fault and I'd know it wasn't me that was the issue. I got back to work, designing on some marketing materials for a new bakery that was opening up in South Carolina (working with small businesses just brought my heart so much joy).

I worked until six, giving myself an hour to look like a decent human being. I told myself that if he stood me up again, I was going to go ahead and still go out and get a drink—I was twenty-eight, I could go have a drink by myself without it being weird. I threw on an outfit and looked in the full-length mirror. The dark-wash jeans made my 5'4" legs look longer, the chunky gray sweater hid my bloating, and some silver jewelry helped to brighten my face just enough. I went into the bathroom and scavenged for a foundation that matched my pale post-winter skin. I swiped some blush on my cheeks to make it look like I had some life in me, put on a pretty nude lipstick, and curled my hair. I examined my average frame, this was as good as it was going to get. As I was walking out of my bedroom, I glanced down at my phone to check the time. I had exactly four minutes to get outside. I made sure everything was in order and placed my hand on the door handle. If Liam was outside, great. If he wasn't, then screw him, it would be *just fine*.

I took a deep breath and turned the handle, exposing my face to the cool late-April air. I looked up, Liam wasn't in sight, go figure. About to resort to plan B, I heard the familiar sound of grass crunching under someone's feet. Key still in-hand, I turned and was met with Liam, standing at the end of my walkway, a bouquet of flowers in his hand.

"Hey, these are for you." He handed over the bouquet of roses. "I really am sorry that I lost track of time. I know it seems suspicious, but I promise, I just tend to get lost in my own world a lot."

I took the flowers, sticking my nose in one of the blooms to take in the sweet scent. "I'm going to put these inside before we go. You can come in if you'd like."

I unlocked the door and was met with a very confused Daisy. I walked through the house into the kitchen and heard the other set of footsteps stop at the entryway, as did Daisy. I placed the flowers on the counter and caught sight of Liam kneeling down, scratching Daisy's stomach, neither of them looking up when I walked over.

"Ready to go?" I asked, eyebrow raised.

"Yep!" Liam stood up, scratching Daisy's head, "It was nice meeting you, Daisy." How did he know her name? Probably because I mentioned it to him when we went out for pizza or because she has a collar on. *Relax, Sadie.* Her tail wagged—that was a good sign that he wasn't going to kill me. I locked back up and we made our way to his driveway, his car already pulled out of the garage and warmed up. He came around to my side and opened the door for me. These gestures were helping his case for proving he wasn't a complete asshole, at least.

I didn't have to give him directions this time. He had pulled up the directions on his phone, so he just followed along and we made it to the bar in no time. This was one of my favorite places to go, it wasn't a raging bar by any means, rather it was more of a wine bar that served some of the best craft cocktails in the state. The atmosphere was warm and inviting. The plush couches were jewel tones, the wooden tables were a deep mahogany, and the lighting was more yellow than bright white. Julia, the owner, greeted us at the hostess stand.

"Sadie! It's been a minute! How are your parents doing?" Julia wrapped me in a hug.

"It has! They're doing really well. How are Paul and the kids?" I always made sure to ask about Paul, her husband. He beat cancer last year.

"They're all doing really well, thanks for asking." She shifted her gaze to Liam and said, "I'm sorry, I don't believe we've met before, I'm Julia, I own The Liquor Lounge with my husband, Paul."

"Hi, Julia, it's nice to meet you. I'm Liam. I just moved here last month." He extended his right hand to shake Julia's. "I'm Sadie's new next-door neighbor."

"Welcome to the area." She escorted us to the couch in the back right corner, the quietest spot in the place. "If you need anything at all, please don't be a stranger. Sadie here is also a fantastic tour guide. Once the weather gets nicer, she should take you on a scenic walking tour of our downtown area. Our city is beautiful when it's not covered in snow or pouring rain." Julia motioned out the window before walking away.

We sat next to each other in awkward silence, off to a great start.

"So . . . what would you recommend I order?" Liam broke the silence exactly three minutes after sitting down.

I looked up from my menu, having already settled on what I was going to order. "Depends on what you like. Did you want wine?"

"I'm not a big wine fan. The cocktails all sound good. Tequila and vodka are my favorite liquors, what would you suggest?"

I thought about it for a second; we have the same preferred liquors, a good sign. "I have two suggestions: the first is a cherry limeade with vodka—it's just the right amount of sweet, tart, and vodka-filled. The second option is ordering the Bartender's Choice. Julia will ask what liquor you prefer, then ask about flavors you do and don't like, and then it's up to the bartender to make something they think you'd enjoy."

I made eye contact for the first time since we got here. Under this lighting, his black hair had a deep shine, his emerald eyes took on a darker hue with a hint of a sparkle, and his olive skin looked even more tan. Bless these lights for making him look even more appealing than he already did.

"Wow, I didn't know that was even a thing. I'm going to start with your cherry limeade suggestion and then I'll do the Bartender's Choice next. What are you going to get?"

I laughed. "A cherry limeade as well. It's my favorite drink here."

He glanced down at his menu again, I knew what he was thinking. "You won't find it on there. It was my Bartender's Choice drink when they first opened and it's my favorite. Every time I come here, that's the first drink I order. Then as the night goes on and I get sick of it, I tend to just start ordering vodka and club sodas with a lime wedge."

I looked up to see Julia was back and ready to take our order. "What'll it be?"

My mouth opened to order, but Liam chimed in before I could speak, "We'll have two cherry limeades with vodka, please."

"Perfect, I'll be right back with waters. Those drinks should be up quickly. If you need anything else in the meantime, just wave me on over."

I smiled as Julia walked away, wondering what in the world we would talk about now that our drink orders had been placed.

"So, have you always lived in Red Oak?" I appreciated what he was trying to do; he was uncomfortable and trying to make small talk. However, this gave me a great way to learn more about him so I could bolster my argument against Audrey when she inevitably asked me what I did tonight. When we went out for pizza, he only gave me a few details of his life, he didn't give me a crash course.

"Yep, born and raised. This tends to be a town where people leave the first chance they get, but not me."

"Have you ever thought of leaving?"

Might as well scare him off with my baggage now. "I have. Before I moved into the rental three years ago, I was in a serious relationship. It's a story as old as time: girl and guy are serious and considering marriage, guy finds a new girl on the side, original girl is left being told that she needs to pack up and move out. I was heartbroken and wasn't sure if I could stand to be in the same state as him." I shrugged, taking a pause. "Then I realized I'd be leaving my best friend, my family, and the town I loved, so I toured the community we live in and have been there ever since."

"I'm really sorry you went through that, I imagine it wasn't easy." His brows were furrowed and he was listening to every word I said.

"It wasn't, but I made it through. Truthfully, you're the first guy I've gone out with since."

"You're not serious . . ."

"Dead serious. I've talked with guys on dating apps, but none of that went anywhere. I found that they were all the same, all boring."

"What tells you that I'm not boring?"

I smiled, he had a valid point. "I don't know that just yet, but I really enjoyed our conversation the other night at dinner."

He met my smile. "I'm happy. But, hearing that I'm the first guy you've gone on a date with in three years is both extremely flattering and terrifying. It makes me feel even worse for the other night. I'm really sorry about that, I'm just surprised that you agreed to go out with me again. I stood you up and didn't deserve this chance. Can I please get your number?" He handed over his iPhone.

"I won't lie, I was pissed off, but there's something about your demeanor that made me feel like it was an accident." I grabbed his outstretched phone and added in my contact info.

We talked for a while more about Red Oak and what there was to do both in the downtown area and if you ventured out to Leeds, before I took the opportunity to pry into his past.

"So, tell me about yourself. Where did you grow up, any hobbies, any weird quirks?" I was getting right to the point.

"I was originally born in Iowa, but my parents divorced when I was three and my mom got sole custody. I'm an only child, so it was an easy ruling by the presiding judge. Once the divorce was finalized, we packed up and moved to Pennsylvania. We were there until I was fourteen, then we moved to Utah. When I turned eighteen, my mom stayed and I moved down to Florida. And that brings us to how I ended up here. My dad and I kept in loose contact over the years, so when he said he was sick and was having trouble taking care of himself, I knew it was time for me to move and take care of him."

"Wow, that's a lot of moving. I'm sure you had lots of different experiences. Is your mom still in Utah?"

His eyes fell, I must have struck a nerve. "My mom passed away three years ago due to complications from surgery."

"Oh, Liam, I'm so sorry. I had no idea otherwise I wouldn't

have asked." I placed my hand on his arm in a poor attempt at comforting him.

"No, it's okay. You had no way of knowing. Even though it's been years, it still stings. Now that my dad is sick, it's just bringing back up all those old feelings of abandonment." He cleared his throat, ready for a change in topic. "As for hobbies, I love a good hike or nature walk, something that came about when I lived in Utah. Are there any good trails here that I should check out?"

"I'm not much of an outdoorsy person myself, but Audrey hikes often. I could ask her for some recommendations for you."

"I'd love that, thank you. If there's an easy trail, would you join me?" Was he asking me out on another date?

"I'm the most clumsy person. If you can handle that and promise to go when there's not snow on the ground, I'll attempt it."

His eyes lit up, I could tell that he didn't often have company on his hikes. "Of course! If you could get the trail info for me, I can plan an entire day for us when the weather warms up. Does the weather, in fact, warm up?" His laugh was raspy, almost melodic.

"It does, usually around the middle of May. We still have a few weeks left of this kind of in-between weather."

"Then it's a date."

I looked down at the table and our two drinks were sitting there, untouched, ice melting. We had been so deep in conversation that we didn't even notice Julia slink over. "We should probably drink those soon." I nodded toward the sweat-covered glasses.

"I hadn't even realized that she dropped them off. They look good." He picked up both glasses and handed one to me as he said, "To new beginnings."

As our glasses clinked, I could feel the walls I had built up start to fall. Not for a second did I think what Liam was telling me was a lie. Just seeing the hurt in his eyes when he was talking about his mom made *my* heart hurt. We chatted for a while and when our glasses were close to empty, Julia came back over and took our next drink order: another cherry limeade for myself and a Bartender's Choice for him. When the drinks appeared, Julia explained that the bartender made a chocolate espresso martini. When it was placed in front of him, Liam smiled like a child waiting to dive into their birthday presents.

By this point, whether it was getting to know him better or the one drink warming me up, I felt myself opening up, giving insight into my more average (than his, anyway) childhood, my friends, what I enjoyed outside of work, and all that fun. He was easy to talk with, his trustworthiness emanated off him like the light from a lightbulb. After our second round of drinks, we agreed it was time to get home, so Liam settled our tab and we were on our way. We stopped at a traffic light and he looked over at me.

"Random question, are you hungry?" It was at that moment my stomach chose to grumble. "I'll take that as a yes. Do you want to come over to my place and we can order some food in? Please don't feel like you have to, I totally understand if you don't feel comfortable."

I briefly thought about it and, *why not*. After all, I'd only be next door, so it wasn't like I would have to drive home late. "That sounds good to me., do you like Thai food?"

"It's one of my favorite cuisines. Is there a restaurant around here?"

"Would I be asking if there wasn't?" I needed to turn the sass down a notch.

He laughed so I knew he understood it was a joke.

"They stop delivering at nine," I said as I glanced at the time on my watch, "and it's already after ten, so I can call and place an order and we can pick it up. We might just need to wait for it for a few minutes if that works?"

"Perfect, can I just have a Pad Thai, please? I'll also need the name so I can punch it into the GPS."

I nodded, giving him the name of the spot, Thai Fusion. While he drove, I dialed the number on their website and ordered our dinner. By the time we arrived at the restaurant, we only had to wait a few minutes before Liam paid and we were back in our community. It was weird walking right by my house and going into his. I wasn't sure why, probably Audrey just getting in my head, but I fully expected his place to be dark and scary-looking. When the door swung open, I was met with light oak furniture and a camel-colored leather sofa and recliner, the exact opposite to what I was expecting. I always found it so weird to see what others did with the exact same space you had. We walked in and I placed the bag of food on the counter while Liam grabbed my coat.

"I can get the plates set up if you'd like to go sit down. There's a blanket on the couch and the buttons to recline are on the side. The remote is on the end table, so why don't you find something for us to watch."

I stared at him, was he serious? He was going to bring me my food? He was letting me pick what I wanted to watch? In the four years I was with Ben, never once was food brought to me, nor was I allowed to pick what show we watched. Reflecting back on that time, it was a toxic relationship and I now knew I deserved better . . . perhaps someone named Liam.

"You're just staring at me, are you okay?"

"Yeah, I'm sorry, this is just new to me is all."

"You being treated this way should be the rule not the exception. Sit down and get comfortable, I'll be right over with the food and some waters."

Was this guy for real? I felt like a princess. I sat down on the side of the couch that didn't have the remote next to it (I figured that was his spot) and made myself comfortable. I was turning on the television when he placed my food and drink on the table, thankful he was there so I could get some input on what he might like to watch.

"I'm lame and usually watch cooking shows."

"Have you seen that new home chef cooking competition show yet?" My blank stare must have given him my answer because he continued, "Last week was the first week and it was really good. I think the second episode has just been added if you wanted to watch that."

I handed over the remote, unsure of what the show was called, and he clicked on the first episode of *Home Chefs Unite* so I could get up-to-speed. Don't get me wrong, the food was good and the show was entertaining, but it was Liam's company and commentary that really made it memorable. We critiqued the people's food like we were Michelin-starred chefs ourselves. I looked down at my phone and noticed that it was already after eleven—Daisy needed to go out once more for the night. I got up to bring my plate and cup to the kitchen, thoroughly impressed by the cleanliness and how nicely furnished it was.

"I have to get back and let Daisy out. I had a really great time tonight, thank you again for both the drinks and dinner, I really appreciate it."

He wandered over to the coat closet and grabbed my jacket, holding it for me while I put my arms through the sleeves. "It was my pleasure. Would you like to do this again next Friday? Drinks, takeout, and the next episode of *Home Chefs Unite*."

"I'd love that! I really did have a great time with you tonight. I'm happy I gave you a second chance." We walked towards the door and he pulled it closed behind us once we were outside.

"What are you doing?"

"Walking you to your door."

"I have to walk across a patch of grass, it's not exactly treacherous."

"I know, I just want to know that you're inside and safe."

We walked the stone's throw to my front door and I unlocked it, ready to go inside and get out of this frigid air. I turned, staring at him. I was so out of the dating realm, I didn't even know what to do. Do I kiss him? Offer a firm handshake? Give a high five? My confusion was all over my face and he leaned in to kiss my cheek, relieving me of any awkward encounters.

"Have a good night, Sadie. I'll talk to you tomorrow."

I walked through the door and waved before closing it. That was one of the best dates I had ever been on, he was courteous, funny, and respectful. Audrey was out of her mind for thinking this guy was sketchy, he just didn't use social media because he liked to be outside and not glued to his phone.

Daisy slobbered all over me, welcoming me home before she bounded to the back door to go outside. I obliged before heading into the bedroom to get changed into something way more comfortable than I had on. Even though it was late, it wasn't too cool out, so I went outside to play catch with Daisy. I flicked on the patio light and looked at the back of the fence to see if anything poked up that could've been what I saw the other night. The only thing was a tree branch. I brushed it off, surely there was a logical explanation for all of it.

We played in the yard for a few minutes before Daisy got bored and wanted to head inside. I made my way to the couch to watch some television. If Daisy didn't need to go out, I would've stayed at Liam's a bit longer since we were enjoying ourselves so much. I reached for my phone to check my emails when I saw it ringing. All the Caller ID said was 'UNKNOWN NUMBER.' I figured it was a late-night spam call so I declined it. A minute later, the same thing happened. I declined it again. Five minutes went by and I thought it had stopped, but I was wrong. If I answered, I could tell them they had the wrong number.

"Hello?"

I was met with a deep voice on the other end of the phone. "Is this Sadie?"

My heart sped up. "Who is this?"

The line went dead and my blood ran cold. Whoever was

on the other end of the phone knew my name. I racked my brain for possible explanations before I fully went into a tailspin. It was probably a prank call. It sounded like the person was using a voice modulator, so it was undoubtedly one of the high school kids in town. I calmed down and went to bed, ready to get out of my own head.

CHAPTER 14

Sadie

SATURDAY MEANT NO ALARM AND NO ALARM MEANT A happy Sadie. Even though last night ended strangely, it was the most fun I'd had in a long time, so naturally, I woke up content with my life's choices. I woke up to the sunshine peeking through the blinds, so I knew as soon as I looked at my phone, I was going to have a text from Audrey asking what I wanted to do today. We weren't glued to each other's hips, but we were just needy enough to have to be up-to-date on everything going on and what the other was doing. I lay there for a few minutes and pet Daisy, thinking about what the day would have in store. Since it was going to be warmer than it'd been, I decided to treat myself to a manicure. I rolled over and reached for my phone to make an appointment. Sure enough, I had messages from Audrey, the most recent being from a half hour ago.

> Audrey: Morning! What are you doing today? It's nice out. Cold, but the sun is out.

Audrey: It's after ten, wake up!

Audrey: Hello? Are you alive??

Sadie: Hey! Later night for me. I was thinking about getting a manicure today. Did you wanna join?

Audrey: Silly question, I'm always down. Late night?

Sadie: I'll make appointments for us for noon if that works. I'll fill you in when I see you.

Audrey: Works for me. Brunch?

Sadie: Want to meet at eleven? That way we have enough time to eat and get over to the salon.

Audrey: Yay! See you then.

I could always count on Audrey to want to go out for brunch at Eggs Up, a new place that opened up last year in Leeds, and get our nails done. I threw on my comfort outfit and washed up and by the time I let Daisy back in, it was time to head out. I drove the twenty minutes there and Audrey was already at a table waiting. She was always way too early for things.

"It's about time you made it!"

"How long have you been sitting here waiting on me?"

"Only five minutes. I ordered us both coffees, they should be right out."

I glanced down at the menu, knowing damn well I was going to order a Californian Eggs Benedict.

"Since I know you don't need to look at the menu, what did you do last night that had you sleeping in and me thinking you were dead in a ditch?"

I inhaled sharply, she wasn't going to like my answer. "It's really a funny story . . ."

She raised an eyebrow. "I like to laugh."

"I told you about Liam and how he just lost track of time, right?"

"Sadie . . ."

"Let me finish! He asked me out for drinks again and I decided to go. It was amazing. We got drinks and he paid. Then we stopped at Thai Fusion and picked up some dinner and then we went back to his apartment and watched a new cooking show."

"You've got to be kidding me. I told you I had some serious concerns about this guy and you still went out with him. And not only that, you went into his house!"

"Here's the thing, I got some background info on him and he's a legitimate person, not in Witness Protection. He moved a bunch with his mom when he was a kid, then moved to Florida. His mom unexpectedly passed away a few years ago and when his dad told him that he was sick, he moved here to take care of him. His dad is in Leeds, which is why we didn't know who he was off the bat."

She stared blankly at me. "I'm still in shock that you went out with him after he stood you up."

Our waitress came over to take our order, a nice reprieve from Audrey's scowl.

"He brought me flowers, so that was a tally in the pro column. He drove. He paid for drinks. He was kind to Julia. He paid for dinner. He also didn't pressure me into going to his house, I willingly entered. When we got in there, he took my coat and told me to go make myself comfortable while he brought me my food and drink."

Audrey looked a little less skeptical. "He sounds like enough of a gentleman." She took a long sip from her coffee mug and added, "I still don't one hundred percent trust him."

"He really was, one of the best dates I have ever been on."

"Better than when Ben took you to Los Angeles?"

"You mean the work trip he took that he brought me along on out of pity? The same one where I sat in the hotel room ninety percent of the time, the other ten percent being when I went out exploring for myself. Yeah, this was much better than that."

"Wow, he really did a number on you. If you're sure about him, then keep going on the dates. I just don't see this ending well."

I knew she had my best interest in mind, but I just wanted her to be happy for me. "I'll see if he texts me today at all, and if he does, see how it goes."

"Whatever you say."

We devoured our food and demolished two coffees each, ready to take on our nail appointment. In Vermont, you wrote off pedicures from November until May because there was a zero percent chance that you would wear an open-toe shoe. When we walked into the nail salon, we were each greeted by name and ushered to our respective nail stations. I opted for a bright purple, while Audrey chose a pale pink. We talked about her parents' upcoming move, what clients I had just taken on, and some upcoming books we were looking forward to. I couldn't help but feel like even though our conversation was normal for us, Audrey seemed weird since I told her about Liam. I knew she wasn't going to be thrilled about it since she already was skeptical of him, but damn, I wish she would've at least pretended to care that I genuinely had a good time last night.

While our nails dried, I checked my phone and had a text from Liam letting me know that he had a great time and that he hoped I had a great day. I made a mental note to text him back when I got in the car to echo his sentiments. When our nails were dry, we parted ways—she went home to do her own thing and I went to the outlet mall to check out the sales. Did I need anything? Most definitely not, but it didn't mean that I couldn't at least look around. If going out with Liam was going to become a more regular occurrence, I'd need some new, nicer tops. Over the last three years, my wardrobe that once consisted of nicer clothes started to dwindle, leaving me with exactly four tops and one dress that were date-appropriate. I swung my bag over my shoulder, heading into the first of many clothing stores.

I spent my afternoon trying on more new tops than I needed, but had no regrets. Did I need six new shirts, a pair of heels, and a new spring jacket? Not one bit, but I sure was happy with my purchases. I loaded all of the bags in the trunk of my car, stopped at the grocery store, and then headed back home just as the sun started to hide behind some rain-filled clouds that were threatening to dump buckets of water down any minute. Somehow, I made it home and let Daisy outside without a droplet falling, and it wasn't until we were both back inside that the heavens opened up. Now that I was home, I could care less the weather had turned; I almost preferred it because it made for a cozy evening. I already knew I wanted to make a pot of white chicken chili for dinner, so this rain was playing right into my plan.

I lit a candle, put on a light-hearted romcom, and headed into the kitchen. I gathered the ingredients, setting them out on the counter, my eyes landing on the flowers Liam had given me. Despite Audrey's concerns, I'd have liked to think that I was a good judge of character—we had an excellent time last night and already had plans to repeat it next week. If I was lucky, we would see each other during the week as well. I didn't have to be lucky, I could have just as easily asked him out as well. Screw it. I reached for my phone and saw I had a text message from him.

Liam: Do you have any plans tonight?

I thought about it, I could invite him over here. I knew I would have enough chili for the two of us, so it was worth a shot. No harm in asking.

Sadie: I don't . . . I was just about to start making some white chicken chili, you're more than welcome to come on over and have some.

97

Liam: What's in this chili you speak of?

Sadie: Well, for starters, chicken. Then onions, jalapeños, white beans . . . all of that deliciousness.

Liam: It sounds fantastic. I'd love to come over for dinner. Do you want me to bring anything?

Sadie: Just yourself.

Liam: Can do. What time?

Sadie: Does 6 work? This takes a little bit of time to cook low and slow.

Liam: I'm free all evening, so just let me know when you'd like me.

Sadie: You can come over and help if you'd like. Not sure if cooking is something you enjoy or not.

Liam: I watch cooking shows . . . I love it. Let me get changed into some real clothes and I'll be over.

Sadie: I'm in sweats and an oversized sweatshirt, please don't worry about looking presentable because I have no plans of getting changed.

I started dicing up the chicken to get it cooking when the doorbell rang, he wasn't kidding about coming right over; not that I minded. In hindsight, the one thing that Ben and I did together that I really enjoyed was cooking dinner on the nights he was home and not traveling for work. He was a financial executive and was gone for two weeks out of each month. It was bonding time for us, but once he ended things, I still continued to cook, using it as my decompression time. I opened the door to a very handsome-looking Liam. He was wearing a fitted navy blue Henley and gray sweatpants. We all know how women feel about gray sweatpants. How did he look even more attractive now, in lazy attire, than he did when he was in jeans and a nice top? He walked in, handing over an unopened bottle of tequila.

"I didn't think wine would be very good with a spicy chili," he said with a shy smile, seeming uncertain of how I would react.

"Oh, tequila! Perfect, I was running low."

"I know you mentioned last night that you liked tequila, so I figured it might be a safe assumption that you had some margarita mix or something."

"Very safe assumption on your part. I make a killer snow margarita, so we can have those. Want one now?" We made our way to the kitchen to get the necessary supplies, this was some serious business.

"A what . . .?"

"Snow margarita! Basically a regular margarita, but instead of adding ice and blending, you just use snow."

"Where are you planning on getting said snow from?" He leaned against the counter with his arms crossed, only seeming slightly concerned that I was talking about snow.

I laughed. "The freezer! Once the snow starts to ease up for the season, I bring a bucket outside and pack it full, then put it in my deep freezer in the garage."

"That's . . . actually genius. Can I help you in any way? If you want to make the drinks, I'm good at chopping. I can get started on that onion."

"Perfect. There's a knife already out, can you do a fine dice on it?"

"Yes, chef."

While Liam diced the onion, I made us a round of snow margaritas, and I had to say, with this expensive tequila, they tasted *so* much better than the ones I normally made. I handed one over to Liam who had finished expertly dicing up that onion and the jalapeños.

He took a long sip. "This is amazing. I didn't even know these were a thing."

"Oh yeah, learned how to make these right after my 21st birthday. They've become a winter staple for me; helps me get through the cold bullshit."

"Well, they're delicious." He swirled his glass. "So, what else can I help you with?"

"Not a whole bunch. I'm going to add in the peppers and onions and let those cook for a few minutes, then I'll add in everything else and we wait."

Once the chili was on the stove and cooking away, we made our way to the couch, finding Daisy sprawled across two cushions. At the sight of us, she knew she needed to get down. We made ourselves comfortable on respective sides of the couch while I found a new movie to put on, something lighthearted and funny, I needed to get the cheesy romance movie off the screen as quickly as possible.

"You don't have to change it, you know." Liam nodded in the direction of the television.

"I've seen this movie so many times, I was just using it as background noise while I made dinner. Do you have any suggestions?"

"We can just talk, you don't have to put anything on for us to watch if you don't want to."

This guy wanted to talk instead of watching a movie . . . This was a first for me.

"Okay," I said after a beat, uncertain of where to start, "I'd love to hear more about what you do for work. I know you said something about computer science, I think that's fascinating."

"I never really knew what I wanted to do with my life when I was younger. I took a year off between high school and college to try to figure life out. While working at a McDonald's, I was the person who fixed all of the registers when they randomly stopped working. It was at that point that I realized I loved all things computers, so I enrolled in college and majored in computer science. Now I work for a tech company as a software developer. The cool thing is I can make my own hours, so when I'm most productive in the evenings, I can get work done and the company doesn't care."

"That's really cool. So do you create the software or fix it? Sorry if that belittled what you do, I'm just ignorant to the tech space."

"Not an ignorant question, very valid. I basically do both. I've come to prefer the building of the software versus fixing it. It's cool to see things come to life from your head, as I'm sure you're aware in your design space."

Finally, someone who understood what it was like to watch things come to life. "Yes! I completely understand that feeling. I've tried to describe it to family and friends before, but I can't eloquently explain it to them. I think it's really cool that you found your passion at a McDonald's in the most unorthodox of ways."

"It was definitely an interesting path to take, but I'm so grateful for it. I don't take it all for granted even for a second. I've had my life flipped upside down multiple times over the course of it, so I wanted some stability."

Now, deeply engrossed in our conversation, time flew by. The next thing we knew, our margarita glasses were long empty and we were in desperate need of a refill. I made us another round and stirred the chili; it was ready. I poured us two bowls, garnishing mine with cheese and sour cream, Liam just adding a little bit of chopped cilantro to his. We ate dinner on the couch because, if we were being honest, no one wanted to sit at an uncomfortable dinner table when the option to recline on a couch was an option.

I held my breath as Liam took his first bite. If he hated it, I knew things would end right then and there. No one wanted to be with someone who didn't like their cooking.

"Sadie," he said, breaking the silence between us, "this is the best chili I've ever had. Did you come up with this recipe?"

"I did." My cheeks flushed.

"This is restaurant quality."

"I make it all the time, I'd be happy to send the rest of this batch home with you." This was definitely evoking confidence.

"No, I don't want to take your food."

"It's really fine, I make this at least once a month and some of it still usually goes to waste. I'd be much happier if you at least took some of it home with you to enjoy another day."

"Well, thank you. I appreciate that."

We went back to eating, focusing our attention on the movie. I glanced over a little bit later and his bowl was empty and he was fully immersed in what we were watching.

"Would you like another bowl?" I asked, starting to stand up, going to put my plate in the dishwasher.

"Oh, I'm full, but thank you. I underestimated how filling it was going to be, that's for sure."

"People usually do, I always send off leftovers for that exact reason."

"I'll take that." He reached for my bowl and brought it over to the sink. "Is the dishwasher clean or dirty?"

As he asked that, my head swung around, he was going to take care of the dishes . . . "Please don't worry about the dishes, just put them in the sink and I can take care of them later."

"Don't be silly; you cooked, I can clean up. You stay right there, nice and comfortable on the couch. I might just need some direction on where to find two containers for the leftovers." He opened up the dishwasher to find it empty, he loaded the dirty dishes and utensils in before I directed him to the cabinet where the plastic containers were. It felt weird having someone else in the house with me again. Aside from Audrey or the occasional visit from my parents, my house was my safe space, my corner of the universe, and I never really let anyone in. The day I moved in, I vowed that this would be my sanctuary, I would stay here as long as I needed to and would build myself back up. I didn't think I would be here for three years, but here we were, and now I had an incredible next-door neighbor who I'd gone out with . . . Been on dates with? Three times now. This was big progress.

While I was lost in my thoughts, Liam had completely cleaned up the kitchen. "Thank you for taking care of that, it wasn't necessary, but I appreciate it."

"Please don't thank me, it's the least I could do. I don't remember the last time that someone cooked for me." He dried his hands on the kitchen towel, folding it when he was done.

Hearing that, my heart sunk. I always took home cooked meals for granted. Whenever I wanted to, I could drive and go to my grandparents' house and get a meal, I could go to my parents' house, or if I really wanted to, I could go to Audrey's parents' house since they accepted me as one of their own many years ago. I made a mental note to bring over more leftovers to him later this week.

"It's getting late, I think I'll head back on over to my place." I glanced over at the clock, it was almost eleven.

I yawned. "That's not a bad idea, I think I'll probably head to bed relatively soon. The rain always puts me right to sleep."

It was Liam's turn to yawn. "You and me both." He reached for the container filled to the brim with leftover chili, "Are you sure I can have this?"

"Don't be silly! It's yours."

"I'll transfer this into a container I have and as soon as I wash it, I'll bring this one back over to you."

"Keep it as long as you'd like, it's a cheap one from Amazon, they're supposed to be disposable, but I try to be somewhat environmentally friendly."

"Only if you're sure." We walked towards the front door.

"Thank you again for the delicious meal and wonderful night. Can I say something that might come off as creepy or too soon?"

My mind raced, not knowing where this was going to go. "Sure."

"I'll start off by apologizing for being this forward, it's very out of character for me." He inhaled sharply before continuing, "I've really enjoyed our time together—these last two nights of just hanging out at home, watching movies, has been extraordinarily fun. I know it's not going out and drinking our faces off in a loud bar, but it feels more intimate, more like I've gotten to know the real you. I really do like you, Sadie, even though we've only technically been on three dates. I know this is really soon, but I tend to fall hard and fast."

My eyebrows shot up, my mouth slightly ajar. "I . . ."

"You don't need to respond, I just wanted to let you know."

"No," I said as I gathered my thoughts, "I actually agree wholeheartedly. At first, I thought you were just some rude guy who wanted nothing to do with me, but I guess I was wrong. I've really had a great time tonight."

A warm smile spread across his face. "You mean that?"

I walked over and planted a soft kiss on Liam's right cheek. "Of course I do. You reminded me what it's like not to be lonely. Somewhere along the way, over the last three years, I became a shell of who I was without even realizing it. I forgot what it was like to meet someone and bond over a good chicken chili." I winked.

"I couldn't agree more. My last relationship didn't end well, so this is a new opportunity for me to do things right."

"Let's consider this a fresh, clean slate for us both." I meant this. I wanted to keep getting to know Liam and spending nights talking and watching cooking shows."

"I should get going for real now, thank you again for a wonderful evening and blowing my mind with this damn chili." He leaned down, his face getting closer to mine, eyes slowly starting to close. As mine closed, I felt his soft lips on mine, an electric shock running through my body. Was this what it was like to kiss someone when you actually had chemistry with them? The kiss lasted but a second before he pulled away. "Goodnight, Sadie. Sleep well."

And just like that, he was gone and I was left alone once again. I locked the door and turned around, facing the rest of the apartment—it felt empty now that it was just Daisy and I. Maybe I did need to find someone and settle down like my mom kept telling me.

CHAPTER 15

Audrey

SADIE MIGHT HAVE BEEN MY BEST FRIEND AND I LOVED her like a sister, but damn, she was stubborn. I really thought that when I started expressing some concerns about this random neighbor that she would back off for a bit while we checked into his background. Normally, I wasn't this crazy and would just let her make her own mistakes, but there was something about this guy that just rubbed me the wrong way. Maybe this was why I dated women: they told you to your face if they didn't like you.

I couldn't put a finger on it, but I had a feeling it was how he stared at her the first time we saw him outside when he was moving in. He looked at her like she was purely an annoyance in his day and from a best friend's perspective, that didn't fly with me. I was going to do everything in my power to check into this guy to make sure he wasn't up to any funny business. I didn't plan on telling Sadie I was doing this unless I found something. I knew she wouldn't be happy with me because she told me to stop, but I just didn't have a good feeling about this guy, or the fact that they had plans again on Friday.

I knew I should just step aside and let Sadie make her own mistakes, but after how things ended with Ben, I couldn't help trying to protect her. Three years ago, I watched her heart shatter into a million pieces when she called me sobbing, telling me that Ben had ended things with her and she needed to move out as soon as possible. From that day on, I vowed to do whatever I could in order to prevent that from happening to her again.

After we got our nails done, I went back to my apartment to start my research for a second time. I hadn't found anything previously, hence my concern, but now I had some more details to go off of. Surely, I'd have been able to find something about this guy somewhere on the Internet. I was now several hours deep into this research and hadn't found anything exciting about this guy. There was no record of him anywhere.

I had a text from Sadie, telling me that Liam had come over for dinner, so I immediately picked up the phone to call her. I hated to admit this, but I grabbed a notebook and pen, ready for any other details she was going to share.

"Hey, Audrey," Sadie answered her phone on the first ring.

"He was over your house? How did this even come about?" I wasted no time in trying to get to the bottom of it.

"Long story short, he texted me when we were getting our nails done. I texted him back and then he asked what I was doing. So, I invited him over for dinner. I made chili, so I was going to have a bunch leftover, it just made sense."

"And how did it go?" She knew I was less than pleased with her for letting this random guy in her house.

"First of all, you can drop your attitude. I know you're not happy that I'm pursuing this, but I need you to just calm it down.

I actually had a really nice time—we had very non-judgmental conversations." She meant that to sting and it sure did.

"I'm sorry, Sadie, I just don't think Liam is who he says he is."

"You just don't want me to be happy for whatever reason. I promise you, he's totally fine. He even showed me pictures from his childhood. He just really tries to stay private."

If he showed her pictures of him as a child, maybe he wasn't so bad. Maybe I *was* overdoing it. "He showed you pictures?"

"Yeah, a few with his mom."

I tried to simultaneously quiz her and fact check myself. "Do you know her name?"

"Are you quizzing me now? Her name was Janice."

That was something for me to go off of. "Wow, this is me waving the white flag, I will stop looking into him."

"Good because he kissed me."

"Excuse me, he did *what?*"

"Before you jump through the phone, it was a peck on the lips. Nothing more. More of a 'good night' kiss between teenagers on a first date."

"Well that's sweet. Did you feel uncomfortable at any point?" I hadn't realized I'd been subconsciously picking at my cuticles, a nervous habit.

I heard Sadie take a deep breath, I braced myself for her long-ass monologue. "Not once. He helped me cook, he cleaned up, we watched a movie. It was just really relaxing. Plus, I enjoyed having someone else around on a Saturday night. That could be my life all the time; I don't have to sit around with only Daisy. I love her more than anything, but I could use a little human interaction in the evenings." She paused, collecting her thoughts. "I could have someone here to help share the load of taking care of the house. I know that sounds silly since it's only 1,500 square feet, but still. I could have someone by my side when I'm cooking. Or, while I'm cooking, he could do the dishes. I know it's still really early on, but

I have feelings of some sort for him. Whether it's long-term or not, he's still someone special that I can spend time with."

Sadie took in a deep breath. "Sorry, I know that was a lot."

I was speechless, I could hear the genuine emotion in her voice.

"You think I'm crazy. Listen, I know . . ."

I cut her off. "No, Sadie, I don't. I can tell you do really like Liam. I'm sorry if what I've done and said has hurt you, I didn't mean it. Please forgive me for overstepping."

"It's okay. I know it wasn't intentional. We're good."

"Cool. I just didn't want you to get hurt again."

"I know, I appreciate that."

We chatted a little bit more, but I could feel myself falling asleep. "I'm exhausted and have to be up early in the morning to help mom and dad move. I'll talk to you tomorrow!"

"Good night."

I ended the call, starting to doubt myself; was I looking into a dead end? I just had a gut feeling that this relationship between Liam and Sadie wasn't going to end well.

CHAPTER 16

Sadie

SINCE I HAD SORTED THINGS OUT WITH AUDREY, I FELT better. She heard my more-than-valid points and might actually leave this one alone. Ever since Ben broke up with me, anytime I'd even remotely mentioned dating someone or even just being interested in them, Audrey went on a wild goose chase to find out absolutely everything about them. She'd helped me avoid some bad ones, that was for sure.

Last year, I had a client that I was doing some design work for and got along wonderfully with. He was the chief marketing officer at a tech start-up and if nothing else, he was very nice to look at—shallow, I know. We worked together for six months and he only lived an hour away, so it definitely could have worked out. That was, until I casually mentioned it to Audrey in passing. She researched him so deeply that she found out his mother's maiden name. She was able to dig up some good information to know, like the fact that he'd been arrested for indecent exposure. Dodged a real bullet there.

I had no hesitations with Liam, last night was evidence of that. If I wasn't comfortable with him, there was no chance in hell that I would have invited him into my home and certainly no chance of cooking for him. I sat on the couch, sipped on a freshly made peppermint tea to help wake me up, and reflected on how well it had gone. Even without me wearing "presentable" clothes, I still felt every bit as secure; maybe even more so because he accepted me when I felt the most unattractive. Daisy whimpered by the front door then. Knowing nothing was out there, I told her to hush her mouth and come hang out with me on the couch. She sniffed the door once more, but happily obliged. It was a cloudy Sunday and I didn't plan on moving from my spot all day.

Hours flew by as I got lost in my tablet—both reading and scrolling aimlessly. I demolished the new romance novel from one of my favorite authors and it was certainly worth the wait, but now I was all up in my enemies-to-lovers trope feels, wondering if Liam was home. I flipped my phone over for the first time in hours to see a text from him.

> Liam: Good morning. Not sure if you were going out anywhere today, but you might want to check your welcome mat.

What in the world was he talking about? I begrudgingly unwrapped myself from my blankets and made my way to the front door. I opened it to find a bag with a bow on it. Now, confused, I brought it inside and placed it on the counter. I carefully untied the bag, peeking in, only to be met with disposable containers, some snacks, and a note.

Sadie –

I didn't feel right just taking a container, so I went to Walmart this morning and bought you an entire pack of them. I'd be lying if I said that this also wasn't a selfish gift. I'm hoping maybe if you have leftovers the next time you cook, you might want to use these to bring some food to 808 Blue Sky Avenue. I hope you have the laziest day ever.Liam

My heart skipped a beat. This was a very thoughtful gift, even if he claimed it was little selfish on his part. I took it as a sign that things were going well between us, even though we hadn't known each other for very long. Sometimes, you didn't need to know someone very long for your heart to catch feelings.

I went back to the couch and typed out a quick response to Liam.

> Sadie: Hey there. Thank you so much for the new dis-posable containers—I'll make sure that they're put to good use. What's your most favorite meal? Btw, you could have rung the bell!

Whatever he said his favorite was, I would to my best to rep-licate it and bring it over to him sometime this week. He must have been near his phone, because he messaged me right back.

> Liam: Any meal I get to share with you is my favorite. And I didn't ring the bell because I didn't want to bother you. I know you said that your goal for today was to do nothing—I wasn't going to interrupt that.

Why does he have to be both extremely attractive and swoon-inducing? If this guy could sing, I would die right there on the spot, happy as can be.

> Sadie: Flattery will get you everywhere lol. If you could have one last meal before you died, what would it be?

> Liam: Some kind of chicken pot pie—something cozy like that.

> Sadie: I see, that's a pretty solid choice.

Liam: What would yours be?

Sadie: I would want to make it myself one last time, but I would choose some kind of broccoli cheddar soup with biscuits. Sounds simple, but it's my favorite.

Liam: Hmm I might just need to try this soup if it's the one you would choose as your last meal.

Sadie: Flatter me enough and I might just make some this week and bring some over to you.

Liam: Is that all it takes? Okay then . . . your hair smells nice, you have the most beautiful smile, you're driven. Shall I continue?

Sadie: Wow! I guess I owe you a bunch of meals now ;)

Liam: Not trying to flatter, just speaking the truth. Now I wouldn't complain if I were to be invited over and meals were prepared.

Sadie: Whoa now, I'll need some assistance if I'm going to be making these meals for two.

Liam: Just call me your sous chef!

This conversation might not mean much to some women, but to me, it was everything. Finding a guy that loved to cook as much as I did was hard to find. The one guy I matched with on Tinder a few years back liked to cook, but he liked to do it alone. Sounded silly, but after he not-so-politely declined my help with cooking, he was going to be taking care of everything alone because I was out of there.

For a split second, I debated asking Liam to come over for dinner, but I didn't want to seem needy. I did decide, however, that whatever I made for dinner tonight, I'd package some up and bring it over and leave it by his front door, just like he did earlier with the containers.

It was still early enough in the day that I had plenty of time before I even needed to remotely start thinking about what was for dinner, but I wrapped myself back up in my burrito and grabbed my iPad, scrolling my way through Pinterest, saving some chicken pot pie recipes. I knew that this was dumb to say, but this guy that I'd known for nearly no time was giving me butterflies already.

I found a pretty straightforward recipe, double checking that I had everything I needed. I didn't have any peas, so that wasn't going to happen tonight, but I added them to my grocery list. I thought on it for a few minutes . . . what if instead of getting take-out on Friday, we made this together? I gnawed the inside of my cheek, debating if I should text Liam and suggest it. I liked him, he seemed to genuinely like me, so why the hell not. For the second time with him, I decided to be brave and made the suggestion.

> Sadie: Hey again. I had a suggestion I wanted to run by you; please feel free to say no . . .
>
> Liam: Oh . . . what is it?
>
> Sadie: I know the week hasn't really started yet, but I had an idea about Friday night's date. What if we go out a little bit earlier, get some drinks, and then we can come back to my place and we can make some chicken pot pie?

Hitting send on that text was a massive hurdle for me. I liked him, too much and too soon, but I was following my gut on this one. The longer it took for him to reply, the more stupid I felt. Five minutes went by, then ten . . . twenty . . . forty . . . an hour. No answer. I re-read what I sent over and over again. I probably scared him off. I put my phone down, maybe if I stopped staring at it, he would respond.

A whole two hours passed before he texted me back. I was in the kitchen sautéing up some veggies to go over rice when I heard my phone beep. I raced for it, nearly throwing myself over the back of the couch in the process.

> Liam: I'm sorry, I must have fallen asleep on the couch. Not ignoring you if that's what you thought! I think that sounds like a great date idea. The weather actually looks like it won't be too nice Friday, so if it's crap, we can skip drinks out and try to make some cherry limeade cocktails at home?

Liam was speaking my love language, the best dates were the ones where you were home, in comfortable clothes, making your own dinner and drinks. While there was a mess to clean up, there was something so relaxing about being in your own space and getting to know someone. I felt like that was definitely the case with us—I enjoyed going out and getting pizza and drinks, but the conversation seemed to flow so much more easily when we were by ourselves in peace and quiet.

> Sadie: Not going to lie, I definitely thought I had scared you away with my suggestion, so I'm happy that I didn't. I think that sounds like a pretty ideal night to me.

> Liam: Not scared away at all, just tired haha

> Sadie: Well that's good to know, I hope your day has been just as lazy as mine has been.

> Liam: The only thing that would've made it lazier would be if you and Daisy were here with me.

> Sadie: I could say the same for you.

> Liam: I mean . . . I could come over and fix that. I can even bring my own blanket since you seem to commandeer them all.

> Sadie: You're more than welcome to. I haven't decided on dinner yet.

Liam: I'll shower and put on fresh sweats and be over within the hour. Don't start cooking without me!

At first, I wasn't sure how this whole living next door to each other thing would go, but honestly, I felt like if you liked the person enough and they respected your boundaries, it was a pretty sweet setup. He could come over whenever he wanted to, I enjoyed his company. I didn't have anything to do until he came over, so I decided to call my grandma since I hadn't spoken to her in a few days. She picked up on the sixth ring—I could guarantee that she had the television on too loud and didn't hear the first five.

"Hello?" my grandma yelled into the phone, *Jeopardy* blaring in the background.

"Hi, grandma!"

"Oh, Sadie! Hello, how was your weekend? Have you seen that Liam guy out and about?"

"So . . . funny story . . ." It took a while, but I told her all the details.

"I guess we misjudged him then, didn't we?"

"Yeah, I guess so. He just seems so down to Earth, if this dating thing doesn't work out with him, I would really enjoy just being friends with him. He has such a kind and warm soul."

"You sound happy and that's all I care about."

"If Audrey had her way, I would have written him off by now. She said that she had a weird feeling about him and said I should steer clear."

"Did you tell her to pound sand?"

"Pretty much, yeah. I told her I was happy and didn't see any red flags with him, so she finally agreed to drop it."

"Do you think she will? Historically, she has a problem with letting things go."

"I actually do think so, she apologized."

"Well good, don't let anyone ruin your happiness."

My grandma was a known gossiper, so I got some good family gossip before my doorbell rang. "That's Liam, I should go get that."

"Go, we'll talk soon! I love you!"

"Love you too, Grandma! Have a great night."

With that, I hung up the phone and made my way to the door, excited for another night at home with my new neighbor.

CHAPTER 17

Audrey

I PLOPPED DOWN ON MY COUCH, EXHAUSTED FROM HELPING my parents pack all day. Sundays were supposed to be relaxing and today had been anything but that. I spent the last twelve hours moving more boxes of clothes than I thought one person could own (thanks, mom). Now, it was time for me to pour myself a glass of white wine and grab my laptop. Just because I told Sadie that I wasn't going to do any more research into Liam, didn't mean I couldn't in my spare time. Something was off with this guy, I just needed to know what.

I tried all of the searches I could think of: Liam Reynolds Vermont, Liam Reynolds Ohio, Liam Reynolds software developer.

Nothing. How did this guy go three decades with no online presence? That just wasn't possible, especially in today's day and age. I clicked on my message thread with Sadie, hoping for some insight. Back when she was on the same page as me with him being weird, she had sent some screenshots of the list of people he was following. I looked through each of them, not finding anything, until I saw "HaileyRL0986." The one person he was following that was an *actual* person outside of the other bizarre accounts, including but not limited to, a McDonald's?. Just looking at his 'following' list, he sure seemed like a sketchy individual.

I clicked her profile, scrolling through her pictures. She looked like a real human being, posting a few times per week until a few weeks ago. I didn't see Liam in any of her photos—it was mostly photos of sunsets, her dog, and her with her friends. I checked to see if she was following him and she was, so clearly she knew him. I grabbed an empty spiral notebook and started taking some notes.

To find out more about her, I knew I would have to go to some pretty sketchy lengths—starting with trying to find one of her friends on Facebook. Since she didn't have a last name on her Instagram profile, I needed to find one of her friends that had their first and last name listed. I scrolled quickly to the middle of the list, Kelly Moran would do.

Next, to Facebook I went. I typed in Kelly Moran into the search bar and hundreds popped up. Why were there so many of them? I thought this was going to be a quick task, I'd done it many times before. The Kelly I was looking for was in Florida—that narrowed it down to only eighty-two results. I clicked the first one, no luck. The second, no luck. I had gone through fifty-seven and had no luck. When I clicked lucky number fifty-eight, I was met with a familiar face. *Finally.* I held my breath, hoping that her friends list was public; my first win.

I scrolled through, looking for a Hailey—there were only three, thank goodness. When I found her I didn't even look at her page, I went straight to her friends list to see if I could find a Liam Reynolds. Two thousand friends and no one by that name. I scrolled through again, looking at the pictures this time. My breath caught in my throat. I clicked a profile with a picture that looked exactly like him . . . but this guy's name was Joe Hale.

I slammed my laptop shut, that was enough research for tonight. What had I just found? I tried to come up with as many possible explanations as I could, but I was failing. Maybe Liam was his middle name or something. Well, that was what I was going to go with. I went to the front door to turn off the porch light and noticed that there was a car sitting in front of my neighbor's house, still running. Normally, I wouldn't have given it a second thought, but my neighbors were out of town this week and next on vacation. I tried not to stare, so I shut off the light and peered out the peep hole. It was a blue car but I couldn't make out the exact model. It looked familiar, but I couldn't place it. I made my way back to the couch and reached for a book to help me get my mind back on track. It was like a lightbulb went off, I knew where I had seen that car before. Outside Sadie's house, the morning Liam moved in . . .

CHAPTER 18

Sadie

I OPENED THE DOOR AND WAS MET WITH A FRESHLY SHOWERED and clean-shaven Liam, one of his blankets draped over his arm. "You look nice." It came out much more surprised than genuine.

"I didn't want to come over in yesterday's clothes again, so I figured I should shower and shave." The right corner of his mouth perked up, a smile threatening to spread across his face as he stepped over the threshold.

I looked down at myself, still very much wearing last night's clothes. My cheeks burned scarlet, immediately self-conscious.

It was evident Liam noticed. "No. Stop that, you look perfect. If you did want to go shower, I could just hang out and see what you've got that we can make for dinner. Unless you were thinking just takeout, in which case, we can definitely do that, too. Your call."

I awkwardly closed the gap between us, placing a kiss on his soft lips, still unsure if that was the right move. "I need to shower regardless, so if you want to hang out with Daisy, I'll be back in like fifteen minutes or so. Make yourself at home."

I headed to my master bathroom, wondering what in the world I was doing—I was leaving my prized possession, Daisy, with a guy I had only known for two months. That wasn't a very long time, if you were wondering. I stood at the bathroom vanity, hands on the counter on either side of the sink, and took in my reflection for a minute. I made note of the smile lines that had started to form around my mouth, the new sparkle of happiness in my blue eyes, my shoulders visibly more relaxed than they'd been. Not for a minute did I think Liam was a sketchy individual—that was all Audrey, who was out of her mind for even remotely believing any of that nonsense. If Daisy was relaxed around him (and she was a really good judge of character) then I knew he had to be a good guy. She didn't hesitate to hide her disdain for others. When the pest control salesman came to the door, Daisy made it well known that she wasn't a fan of random people turning up. It turned out that it actually was a scam, so she was right on the money.

Feeling comfortable with my decision, I turned on a playlist I had created that was solely comprised of relaxing songs. I made my way to the shower, turning the knob to the hottest setting the water would go. I was one of those people who, if I didn't come out of the shower with red splotchy skin, I wasn't happy. I shimmied out of my old sweats and hopped in, letting the beads of hot water hit my neck and run down my back. I was lost in my own world, filled with music and showering, when I heard a loud boom. I knew it hadn't come from inside; from the way the walls vibrated, that was thunder. I sketchily reached out of the shower to check my phone, drying my hand on the shower curtain. Met with a severe thunderstorm alert, I knew Daisy was going to be a handful tonight.

I continued my shower, albeit speeding up, hearing the

occasional loud clap of thunder. As I was washing the conditioner out of my hair, eyes closed, there was a rumble of thunder like I had never heard before and the water ran cold as the lights cut out. My bathroom was completely dark except for my phone that was on the charger. As soon as the power cut out, my phone stopped charging and the screen illuminated. I froze in place.

I jumped, hearing a gentle knock at the bathroom door. "Hey, are you okay in there?"

My voice shook as I called out, "Yeah, I'm fine. I'll be right out."

"Do you need a flashlight so you can see?" If things didn't work out between us, I would still use Liam as a litmus test for all other guys going forward.

"No, I have my phone, I should be good."

"Did you want me to wait outside the door for you with a proper flashlight?"

I tried to steady my racing heart. "No, it's okay, I'll be fine."

"Daisy is here with me, we'll wait for you right here. Be careful stepping out of the shower."

I slid the curtain back, realizing I didn't have a bath towel in there with me. All of my clean towels were in the laundry room, folded in the basket. Shit.

"Hey, Liam, are you still out there?" My voice was low, still only mildly shaky.

"I am, you okay?"

"I just, um . . . forgot a towel . . ."

"I can get one for you, where are they?"

"The laundry room. There's a basket of them in there. Just one will be fine, please."

"Hang tight, I'll be right back."

I stood there awkwardly, naked in my dark bathroom, waiting for a guy I didn't know overly well bring me a towel.

"I'm back, towel in hand. Why don't you get back in the shower and close the curtain? I'll put the towel on the counter.

Be careful." This guy was the master at being respectful. I did as he said and got back in the shower, the door cracking open slightly, a towel was placed on the vanity for me.

"Thank you," I called from behind the curtain.

"My pleasure. There's also a flashlight on top of the towel." He was too good to me. "I'll be waiting for you right out here."

To anyone else, that would've sounded creepy, but to me, it was comforting. It was nice being the one taken care of instead of being the caretaker. When I was with Ben, I always did the laundry, set out his suits for him (his odd request), basically acted like his mother. Now it looked like it was my turn.

I grabbed the flashlight, shining it up at the ceiling for some light to cascade down while I was getting changed. I took note of the towel—it was my favorite purple bamboo one. How did he know it was my favorite? I knew it wasn't on the top of the pile. My heart started to pound, thinking back to Audrey's concerns.

You don't even know that much about him.

I shook it off, I knew I was getting in my own head. I finished drying off, slipped into my fresh lounge pants and sweatshirt, and opened the door. I found Liam sitting cross-legged on the floor, Daisy's big head in his lap, her ears being stroked.

"She seemed anxious, so I figured maybe sitting on the floor with her might help. Is she normally like this or is it just because she was with me when it started storming?"

My heart sped up again, but for a different reason this time. Seeing him on the floor with Daisy, calming her down the only way he could, made my heart happy. Just the sight made any concerns I briefly had melt away.

"She's always like this when it storms; doing exactly what you're doing is one of the only things that calms her down. If I have enough notice that a storm is going to roll through, I get these little CBD squares that I give her and they work like a charm."

"That's good to know. Did you want to take my place and I can go get one for her?"

"You stay put, I'll go get one." I walked over to the pantry and grabbed a square out of the container, returning moments later. I knelt down next to Liam and Daisy and hand-fed it to her. Since they were all-natural, they only took a few minutes to kick in. We sat in the dark, on the floor in silence while she visibly relaxed.

"Hey, I think she's asleep, do you want me to carry her to her bed?" he asked, just above a whisper.

"Oh." I didn't know what to say. "I mean, you can just get up, she can just sleep right here on the rug. She'll be fine."

"But she would be more comfy in her bed."

I was happy the power was out because Liam couldn't see the blush creep up my cheeks from all the swooning I was doing at the moment. A smile danced on my lips.

"She definitely would."

He got up, holding her head while he moved, careful not to wake her. I thought he was going to heed my suggestion of just leaving her there, when he crouched back down, carefully picking her big body up. He carried her across the room and placed her down on her plush bed, giving her head a good pet before getting back up and walking over to me. I think I just died and went to heaven.

"Thank you for that. I know she can't say it, but she appreciates it. She's always been so anxious when it storms, it's so sad to see. It took forever to figure out something that would help her settle." We sat down on the couch, the lights still off.

"Poor thing." He paused for a moment, "So . . . dinner . . ."

"Well, anything that requires cooking of any kind is out." I thought about what I had in my pantry and produce in my refrigerator.

I chewed on my thumb nail, thinking of a solution. Within two minutes, I had a plan. "Alright, hear me out. I have canned chicken, celery, onion, apple, mayo. I can make a chicken salad. I also have a French baguette, so I can cut that up and we can either dip the bread or top the bread with the chicken. Thoughts?"

"I think that sounds delicious. I can tell you watch a lot of cooking shows, though."

By the tone of his voice, I wasn't sure how to take that. Was he complimenting me? Or was he mocking me? "Yeah . . ."

"No, that's a good thing. I'm really impressed that you didn't suggest a peanut butter and jelly sandwich."

"Do you want to start this process now? It could take a while in the dark."

"Do you have candles?"

"What?"

"Candles—do you have them? We could light them so we don't have to hold the flashlights. Unless I'd be best used as the sous flashlight holder."

I thought about it, I knew if I had a light, I could make this pretty quickly. And, judging by how loudly Liam's stomach grumbled, he had to be starving.

"Would you mind holding the light, my sous chef? I can make it quickly and I could hear your stomach a minute ago . . ."

"I can do that." He was enthusiastic about holding a light for me while I made the freaking chicken salad.

We went over to the kitchen and fell into a natural rhythm. Liam handing me things I needed while holding the light, me chopping and mixing, making the chicken salad. Within a half hour, our dinner was ready and we were back on the couch, rain still pounding on the roof. Since there was no television or any other distractions, we were left to conversation in the dark.

It started off awkward, I wasn't going to lie. We talked about the rain and not much else, then we started a more natural conversation. He asked extensively about what my college courses had been like, what my favorite design I had ever done was, what big corporations were terrible to work with, and how my design process worked. It was so nice to get to talk to someone about my job who showed a genuine interest. Since we grew up together, Audrey never really showed much of an interest in my graphic design, which I don't fault her for.

"Tell me about you." I finally spoke up after a few minutes of silence.

"What do you want to know?" His voice was huskier now that it was pitch-black, the only light was coming from some candles on my entertainment center.

"Tell me about your mom . . . if you want."

"I can do that." He spoke for a while about her—how great she was, how she loved him, funny things she used to say. I could tell after a few minutes that it was getting harder to talk about her without getting more sad, so I asked him about his job. He droned on about coding, and what cool new tricks he learned, and *blah blah blah*. It wasn't that I didn't care, because I really did, it was just that he was using words that were foreign to me, so I only understood a fraction of it. I muttered some "mhms" and "oh wows" accordingly though, not to worry.

We were silent for a while, I kept moving closer for warmth because no power meant no heat, and no heat meant the inside temperature was dropping and quickly. We were cuddled together under three blankets when he finally spoke up.

"Hey, Sadie."

"Yeah?" I was sitting to his left, snuggled between him and the couch, facing away from him.

"Can I ask you a question?" He paused. "It's going to be weird, but I just have to know if I'm crazy or not."

"Of course."

"When we're together, do you feel like the world quiets down, and everything is blocked out?" He paused, taking in a deep breath before he said, "I really enjoy when we're cooking together—I love to see the concentration on your face. Did you know that when you concentrate really hard, you stick the tip of your tongue out? I know I'm rambling and that this is probably more cringey for you than it is for me, but I just needed to get this off my chest. I know we haven't known each other for long, but I feel like with you, with everything you've shared with me, I've known you for longer." I could feel his heart racing.

"I know exactly what you mean." I snuggled in closer, resting my head on his toned chest, taking in his musky, outdoorsy scent.

"So would it be super weird if I asked you what we were? Like, are you planning on dating other guys? Or are you talking with them?" I could hear the anxiety in his voice.

"I was wondering the same thing. I really enjoy all the time we spend together and wasn't planning on talking with anyone else. I don't know if we should put a label on us after four official dates, but I think we're heading in the right direction." I tilted my head up to look at his face, my eyes focused on his plump lips.

"Then this is an extraordinarily convenient housing situation we've got here." A smirk was playing at his lips, given away completely by the twinkle in his eye.

"Oh, is that so?"

"It certainly is."

I inched my face closer to his. "Why is that?"

"You know, just convenient for meeting up."

"Right, I definitely believe that." The tension in the air was thick enough to be cut with a knife; one of us was going to have to make a move. I took on that responsibility, knowing Liam wasn't the type of guy to push himself on a woman, evident by the small peck on the cheek.

This would be my first time in years. I had refused Audrey's insistence that I download some dating apps and hook up with random guys—you could call me old fashioned, but I preferred to meet guys in-person, just so I could tell if there was chemistry or not. All the other guys I'd attempted to date over the last three years were spiked down by Audrey, so now that I had finally found a good guy, one that I connected with on another level, I was seeing green flags across the board. I was *more* than ready.

I snuggled in closer to Liam's side, inhaling his warm, woodsy scent. "So, since we still don't have electricity, what do you want to do to pass the time?"

"We can watch a show or something on my phone, if you'd like. Or, I could go back to my place and grab my iPad—I have the cellular option, so we can stream something on there." He was so sweet, his mind not even remotely where mine was at; I needed to be a little more forward. Gosh, this was so awkward.

"I mean, or we could occupy our time another way . . ." I trailed off, both my eyebrow and corner of my mouth were raised, hoping he would catch my drift.

"Oh, I see." The candle flickered and the light caught his eyes, hungry with desire.

I didn't intend on this happening while we were in a downpour and had no electricity, not to mention me being in the most unattractive clothes I owned, but this was happening by light of candle. I shifted so my chest was pressed firmly against the side of his torso, closing the small gap between us. He took the hint and he found my lips.

CHAPTER 19

Liam

I LOOKED DOWN AT SADIE AS SHE SNUGGLED IN CLOSER TO my side, her eyes closed. Her wet blonde hair framed her angular face perfectly. I nuzzled my nose into it, inhaling her wildflower-scented shampoo. The power was still out, so the only light was the soft glow from the lit candle which illuminated her face beautifully.

At some point after our escapades and during our cuddling session on the couch, we fell asleep, because we were awoken by the sound of the microwave beeping, indicating the power had just come back on. Some of the lights were still flicked to the 'on' position, so the house lit up like the sky on the Fourth of July. I was temporarily blinded before I got up without a word and turned most of them off.

Sadie sat up and grabbed her phone, checking the time, it was a little after one in the morning. "I think it's time for bed. I have some early morning client calls." Her voice was thick with sleep.

I made my way back to the couch, grabbing the blanket I had brought over. "I'll head out now."

"You can stay if you want. I wasn't kicking you out."

"No, it's best if I head home, you go get some sleep. Do you need anything before I leave?"

The corner of her mouth twitched up in a mischievous way when she said, "I mean . . ."

A smile spread across my lips. "You're trouble." I wanted nothing more than to stay, but was trying to do the gentlemanly thing and leave.

"I am not!" she rebutted, arms crossed across her chest.

"You most certainly are. Now, you lock the door, okay?"

She pouted like a petulant child. "Fine."

We made our way to the front door, exchanging a hug that lingered a little too long. I knew that I need to go, but there was just something about her that pulled me in. I kissed the top of her head.

"Get some rest, we'll talk tomorrow." I gave her a quick kiss and ushered myself out the door. I stood there for a moment, waiting until I heard the click of the lock before walking away. That was a big perk of living next to the girl I was seeing . . . Well, that was weird to say. I hadn't had a girlfriend in a good long while, let alone bonded so quickly with another person. I knew it was early and I shouldn't have said anything, but I just couldn't not say it when I felt it so strongly. I didn't even recognize who I was anymore.

Earlier when I carried Daisy over to her dog bed in the bedroom, Sadie didn't think I noticed, but I could hear the appreciation in her voice. I'd never felt appreciated like that before. This was all I'd ever wanted in life—to feel wanted and needed. But, no matter how great I felt about us, I knew what I was hiding from her and the rest of this town; I knew what was at stake here.

I shuffled in bed in the morning, unable to muster the energy to get myself moving for the day. The rain was still lightly beating on the windowsill. I replayed all of last night's events over and over in my head, going mad. It went the way I'd wanted it to, but still, it sounded too emotional. From a young age, my mom always told me that I should mask my emotions in front of others. That was why, a few years ago when my dad passed away, everyone else was crying and I just stood there, never lowering the mask that covered up how distraught I was.

It took an hour and lots of scrolling on my phone, but I finally got out of bed and made my way to the kitchen. It was a rainy Monday and I had no job and no job prospects. I debated texting Sadie to say good morning but I didn't want to be needy and didn't want her to know that I didn't have a job. I played it off as working whatever hours I wanted to, but in reality, I was unemployed and had been for a while.

I was making a fresh pot of coffee to help breathe life into my body when I heard my phone vibrate on the couch cushion. It was inevitably just an email, so I ignored it and continued on my coffee venture. Once my fresh cup was poured and the first sip hit my tongue, I dropped my coffee off on the end table, then made my way to the office to grab a new book off the shelf—my typical morning routine. When both of your parents were dead and you had no family around, you tended to escape into books to pretend your life was something it wasn't.

I was big into thrillers. They were one of the only things that made my heart race and made me feel somewhat alive.

Before Sadie, I did a lot of things I wasn't proud of, becoming a shell of a person. I vowed to be better here, do better, but I didn't know how much longer I could keep this façade up. I didn't know how much longer until my past caught up to me and ruined my present.

CHAPTER 20

Sadie

THIS MORNING WHEN I WOKE UP, I WAS GENUINELY HAPPY for the first time in a long time. Not that I wasn't happy being alone, because I was; it was just nice that I could have the only guy I'm seeing over. I wasn't sure I'd be getting used to saying that anytime soon. I thought that was what always made me the most upset about the break-up with Ben—the loneliness I felt at night when the house was quiet and I could hear every creak. You didn't understand paranoia until you lived alone for the first time.

I sent Liam a good morning text, not caring at all if it was too forward. When he didn't reply right away, I took this as my sign to get up and get my day started. I had a few client discovery calls this morning—three of which went really well, only one who stated that my prices were just way too high. Once the three contracts were signed, I would be fully booked for the first time ever. I dedicate a certain number of hours per week to each client, so once these were signed up, my week was full. A new boyfriend *and* my little design business had me working full-time hours? What an amazing twelve hours.

I kept my head down most of the day, focusing on getting my more administrative stuff done since month-end was rapidly approaching and I had to pay taxes and get everything in order. I noticed around two that Liam still hadn't texted me back and figured he was busy with work, so I didn't worry. Around 4:30, he finally texted back, and it was only then that I realized that my shoulders were tight with the same anxious feeling that coursed through my veins every time Ben would be on a work trip with his model-looking co-workers and would leave my messages on read for days before responding.

I knew I hadn't known Liam for all that long, but the conversations we'd had were already deeper than any of the ones I ever had with Ben. The two of them were like night and day. Ben was closed-off and only cared about himself, Liam was kind and courteous. I knew that I would do whatever I could to make this relationship work out. He lived next door, was an awesome sous chef, had a great job as a software developer, and was glorious to look at—all of those were in the pro column if you asked me.

I had been staring outside at the light rain for longer than I thought because it took my phone vibrating again for me to snap out of it. It was Audrey asking me what I was doing for dinner tonight. I responded to Liam first and filled him in on my day since he asked. I thought about my dinner prospects: stay home and eat alone, Liam could come over and we could cook, or, I could go out and get Mexican food at Los Amigos with Audrey. As much as it would be nice to stay in my sweatpants, I knew that a margarita and chips and salsa were calling my name. I texted her back telling her that I would meet her at six and finished up my work for the day.

Liam was wanting to come over and hang out again, but I

knew starting a relationship off being together nonstop was probably not the healthiest, so I told him I was getting dinner with Audrey. I had to say, it was nice to feel wanted for once.

I closed my laptop, took a quick shower, put some real clothes on, and called it good. I met Audrey at the restaurant right at six and they seated us right away. We went there often enough that they knew we didn't need to look at the menus, so once we were seated, our server and the restaurant owner, Ángel, went ahead and took our order.

Something was up with Audrey, she just seemed off, so after a few minutes and a couple of awkward sips of my margarita later, I spoke up.

"So, how was packing your parents' house?"

"It was fine, we got everything in the bedroom packed up, including my mom's closet, they just have the kitchen left to pack. Which, if you ask me, is the worst part." She laughed, but I could see she was hiding something. That was what twenty-five years of friendship did—you could see through the other person's bullshit.

"Packing is, without a doubt, the worst part."

No response. Not even an acknowledgment of what I had just said. It was like Audrey was off on another planet.

"Are you okay?" I asked, worried something was wrong.

"Yeah, I'm good. Sorry, just a long day."

I didn't believe it, but I let it slide. She would crack and tell me eventually.

"So, what's new with you?" I was just making awkward small talk at this point to get through the dinner. I would have never come if I knew that she wasn't going to be in a talkative mood.

"Not much, what's new with you?" Audrey showed no emotion on her face except concern.

"Well, I do have some news. Liam and I are kind of officially dating. And before you say anything, I know it's soon and all that, but I really do feel like I have a deep connection with him."

"What do you mean by 'kind of dating'?" Audrey's eyebrows furrowed.

"We don't want to put a label on it because it's too soon, but we both don't want to date other people. We fully recognize that we haven't known each other very long and we've only been on a few dates, but we want to see if this works out."

"You've got to be kidding me. I told you the other day that I had apprehensions about this guy, and still very much do, and you just go ahead and jump into a relationship with him. Absolutely asinine, Sadie."

Her words stung. We had gotten into arguments over the course of our lifetime, but this felt different. I was genuinely happy with all aspects of my life for the first time in years and she was trying to rip that away from me.

Tears pricked the corners of my eyes. "Why don't you want me to be happy?"

Her eyes softened a bit. "It's not that I want you to be unhappy, Sadie, I just don't know that I trust everything Liam has told you."

"When don't you have concerns about someone I have a remote interest in?" I spat back at her.

"And look how they've all panned out. The one guy was a streaker!" She paused. "Listen, I think that maybe you just need to take a step back for a minute and be objective about this. You don't even know this guy! And I've been your best friend for a quarter of a century."

I knew deep down she had my best interest at heart. "Have you been doing more research on him?"

Audrey's eyes darted down, she had.

"I mean . . . not a whole lot."

"I thought I told you to stop. I wanted to find out things about Liam on my own—without your help." My voice was firm. I caught the attention of Ángel and asked him for my food to go. Audrey stared at me.

"You're leaving? Sadie, we haven't even eaten yet."

"I'm not going to sit here and be judged my entire meal. I'll take it home and eat in peace." I felt like I was acting like a child, but this was the only way to get out of this situation in a civilized manner.

"I'll stop, I promise. I'm sorry, I just can't stand the thought of you getting hurt again. When things exploded with Ben, I was there every day with you. I was your shoulder to cry on, the one who brought you ice cream, the one who did everything for you. Excuse me for just trying to ensure that doesn't happen again." Her voice was stern.

"I know, but this one feels different."

"You've said that about all the others, though."

"I know I have, but this one really is different. He's shared so much about himself over the last few weeks. We've bonded over our love of cooking, thriller novels, and so many other things."

Audrey scoffed. "Sure, whatever you say. Believe what you will."

Our food was being brought over to the table, Audrey's on a plate, mine in a Styrofoam take-away container. I chugged the last two sips of my margarita, paid my bill, and left without another word. As I was walking out the door, I could feel her eyes burning holes in my back and I knew why. I'd never had the confidence to stand up to her, I always took what she said at face value. And for the first time ever, I was standing my ground.

By the time I was in my car and on my way home, I felt the hot tears I had tried so hard to keep in spill down my cheeks. I knew I had overreacted and should have probably listened to Audrey's concerns, but at this point, I just wanted to be left alone. I opened the garage door and pulled my car in, not wanting to interact with anyone else tonight. Daisy met me excitedly at the door and when I crouched down to her level, she sensed something was wrong and licked the salty tears from my face. There was something so comforting about her, she always made me feel better, even in my worst hours.

Now fully in a foul mood, I heated up my bean and rice burrito (extra queso on top, guacamole and lettuce on the side), in the microwave and made it to my spot on the couch. Just as I'd found a show to watch, and taken my first bite of deliciousness, my phone buzzed. I rolled my eyes, it was probably Audrey wanting to talk things through and I was in no mood, so I left my phone face down on the couch cushion next to me. Ten minutes later, another text. Ignored. Five minutes after that, another text. Starting to think that something might be wrong with a family member, I checked my phone. No messages from Audrey (a little surprising), but they were all from Liam.

> Liam: Hey, just heard your garage door close. You've not been gone very long, did everything go okay with Audrey?
>
> Liam: I'm sorry if something happened between you both.
>
> Liam: Sadie, you there?

My brow furrowed, I wasn't used to someone caring about my whereabouts like this before. I willed myself to not let it throw me off, he probably meant it to be endearing. He knew I was going out for dinner, noticed that I wasn't gone for very long, put two and two together, and figured something must have happened between us. He wasn't wrong, but I wasn't going to tell him that. I didn't need him getting protective over this, when by the end of the week, it'll have blown over.

I texted him back to tell him that everything was good, I just wasn't really in the mood to be out for very long. He immediately texted me back that he would come over and keep me company while I ate my dinner. How could he know I didn't eat at the restaurant with Audrey, just quickly? I told him that I just wanted to sit and read a book tonight (not a lie) and that I would talk to him in the morning. I was still slightly thrown off by how he seemed to know so much from so little information. With Audrey acting weird and now Liam wanting to suffocate me while I ate my damn burrito, my irritated mood intensified and was now annoyed with everyone.

I put my phone on silent mode and flipped it over. I focused my attention back on the television while I ate, then switched over to my book. Why couldn't anyone just let me enjoy my damn burrito.

I had a lot of pent-up anger, so as a way of relaxing, I organized my office. I pulled all of my books off the shelf and found one that I didn't recognize. It was a copy of It by Stephen King. While I loved most all of King's novels, I just couldn't stomach that one. I could listen to true crime all day but give me a clown and I was scarred for life. I examined it closer, it definitely wasn't my book. I embossed the title page of each book and this one definitely didn't have that, nor would I have ever picked it up. I looked at the spine and noticed a small red light in the title on the cover. I wasn't sure if it was a camera or not. Where had this book come from and why was it recording me? How long had it been here?

The only people that had been in my house were Audrey and Liam. My stomach flipped and I was immediately unsettled. Someone had set up a camera in my office. I didn't know who was on the other end, but I was terrified.

I thought back to all the conversations I'd had in my house within the last week and there was nothing worth recording. I was a very unexciting human being, whoever placed this here wanted to know my every move. I thought back to the car that was sitting outside when the security footage cut out. Was whoever I'd seen peering over my fence the person who left this book here? That seemed impossible because I didn't leave the house very much . . . but I did leave for dinner. I checked the security footage and there was nothing there. My heart raced and I took the book into the garage and left it out there until I could come up with a permanent solution.

While I knew putting the book in the garage was the right move, I was unsettled that whoever was on the other side of the camera would know I now knew. I picked up the phone and called the police to report it. Unfortunately for me, there wasn't much they could do and told me to call back if anything else happened.

I settled for the next best thing and called Liam.

"Hello?" He was confused because I had just told him I wanted to be alone tonight.

"Hey, random question for you."

"What's up?"

Your girlfriend might have completely lost her mind.

"Have you ever read the book *It* by Stephen King?" I tried to keep my voice level so he wouldn't pick up on the anxiousness bubbling up.

"Nope, I haven't. Why?"

"Just wondering was all."

"You called just to ask me about that book? Wouldn't a text have sufficed?" I didn't blame him, this was a strange call to make. I should've just sent a text, but my anxiety wouldn't allow for that.

"Yeah, that was it."

"Sadie, what's going on?"

I inhaled deeply, running through the last twenty minutes of my life. Still on the phone, the doorbell rang.

"It's just me." I heard simultaneously through the phone and the door. I opened the door to find Liam standing there, looking like a disheveled mess.

"How long ago did you find it?" He growled, shoving his phone in his pocket and made a beeline for the garage.

"Within the last hour."

He barreled through the door that led from the kitchen to

the garage. He grabbed the book, examining it. "Have you checked your security cameras?"

I nodded. "Nothing except the two of us."

I feel like my house was no longer mine. Someone had been in here—potentially while I was home—and was spying on me. They were watching me work for hours each day. They saw me doing stretches mid-day. They had learned my habits and routine.

I thought back to everything that I thought I heard and saw and the feelings of uneasiness over the last month or so. Anytime I felt like I was being watched, it was because I was . . . just on a camera. My house didn't feel safe anymore.

CHAPTER 21

Audrey

O NCE I FINISHED EATING MY TACO PLATTER, I PAID MY
tab and headed home, absolutely appalled by Sadie. How
rude of her to storm off on me like that. I was just trying
to protect her from this guy who might not be who he said he was.

It'd been two weeks since I started digging into Liam behind
Sadie's back and one week since the dinner fiasco at the Mexican
restaurant. I wanted nothing more than to text Sadie and tell her
that he wasn't who he said he was. But, I told her that I would stop
looking into him, so I needed more evidence before I brought it up.
I sat down at my kitchen island and reached for my laptop—all the
browser tabs were still open; Liam's face plastered on my screen.
My stomach lurched, I couldn't believe what I had stumbled upon.

Disgusted by Liam's face, I clicked the back button, only to be met with Hailey's. Since I was only using her to find Liam, I didn't think there would be any relevant information on her profile, but scrolled, regardless. My jaw dropped. Her profile was filled with posts from two weeks ago from friends and family saying how they couldn't believe that she had just been found and how tragic this all was. My heart raced in my chest. Two weeks since . . . what? I scrolled farther down the page, my eyes growing wider with each post. Slowly putting pieces together, I knew I needed to consult Google.

I typed Hailey Rae Lewis into the search bar and hesitantly pressed enter. I was met with news articles from all over the state of Florida. My eyes watered and my palms were sweaty reading the details of her case.

Hailey Rae Lewis, 24, of Tampa, Florida, was reporting missing three years ago on October 14 by her boyfriend, Joe Hale. Her parents, Ronald (Ron) and Amelia (Mia), suspected foul play, but over the last three years, Hailey was frequently posting on her Instagram account. While citing that they had lifestyle differences with their daughter, Ron and Mia eventually came to believe that Hailey packed up her essentials and left town to start a new life.

Two weeks ago, a little more than three years after she went missing, Hailey's skeletal remains were found on a small private beach in Tampa. The forensic anthropologist's preliminary findings on the remains has been conducted and an accidental death was ruled out. Hailey sustained over ten stab wounds to her chest and abdomen, most likely her cause of death. This is still a developing case and this story will be updated as more details emerge.

I could barely finish reading that article before my stomach lurched. There were so many things that needed answers. Liam's real name was Joe? Joe was Hailey's boyfriend? Why did her parents suspect foul play? What lifestyle differences did she have with her parents? Who was posting on behalf of Hailey the last three years? What in the world was going on?

I knew this was serious and that I shouldn't have been doing research on my own, but since no one else was digging, I was going to. I needed to protect my best friend from this guy who had been clearly lying to her and manipulating her for the last few months. The smell from the fresh pot of coffee that I had brewing was making me nauseous after everything that I just read. I dumped the full pot into the sink and rinsed it down the drain.

After I took a walk around the block to clear my head, I grabbed a glass of water before heading back to my spot at the kitchen counter, ready to start digging into Joe Hale, despite my quickening pulse. We weren't playing around with a tech giant who, at thirty-eight, still slept in Rugrats sheets. No, we were dealing with someone who might have killed his ex-girlfriend. I needed more facts before I went to Sadie, let alone the police. If I went with a hunch, they would laugh in my face.

I opened my notebook to where I had left off and focused my attention on my blank laptop screen. When I left my apartment, I had eight tabs open and now . . . nothing. While it was weird, I figured my laptop had just restarted on its own.

Shaking off any potential thoughts, I dove straight back in and looked at the facts. To start, I drew out a massive web across a sheet of lined notebook paper, connecting people, places, and times—my full intention was to fill it in as I gathered more information.

I focused my efforts on Liam for today, figuring that it was the perfect place to start. Wait . . . Joe, I had to remember to call him Joe from now on, at least in my notes. I needed to be careful when talking with Sadie. The more information that I could gather on him, the better. I needed to learn everything about him before I ruffled any more of her feathers. I opened up a new browser and typed in Joe Hale . . . curious to see what came up. First search result: an obituary for his father, Joe Liam Hale, Sr. My eyes widened as I clicked the article.

"What in the world . . ." I said aloud, no one there to hear me.

My first reaction was to pick up the phone and call Sadie, but I fought the urge to do so. I would tell her everything once I had some more concrete information on him. I continued reading the obituary—it went into detail about how he was a well-loved man, his career as a carpenter, and so on. The more I read, the more confused I was. Joe told Sadie that he moved with his mom out to Pennsylvania after his parents' divorce when he was three. These dates told me his parents didn't get divorced until he was . . . fourteen. More confused than when I started this journey, I added that piece of information to my notebook.

To ensure I was keeping all of the information straight in my head, I decided to write out all the information Sadie had willingly given me.

Notes:

- Joe Hale (Liam Reynolds) was originally born in Iowa, parents divorced when he was three, mom got sole custody.
- Once his parents' divorce was finalized, they moved to Pennsylvania. There until he was fourteen, then moved to Utah.
- When he turned eighteen, Mom stayed and he moved down to Florida.
- He and his dad kept in loose contact over the years, but recently his dad became very ill, so he moved to Vermont to take care of him.
- Mom passed away three years ago due to complications from a surgery.
- He loves cooking.
- He "really likes Sadie" and now they're dating.

I knew I needed to apologize to Sadie for how things ended at dinner last week, but I didn't know if she was willing to talk with me yet. To be fair, I didn't blame her. I did step out of line a little too much, but, she should have been thankful that I started my research because I might not have stumbled upon the fact that this guy wasn't who he says he was and that he (allegedly) killed his ex-girlfriend.

I'll give her until the middle of this week, if I don't hear from her, I'll text her.

CHAPTER 22

Sadie

AFTER LAST MONDAY'S NONSENSE WITH AUDREY, I WAS in no rush to talk with her. A week and a half have gone by and like clockwork, she just texted me, asking what I was doing tonight. That was one thing about Audrey, she'd never had many friends so she always stuck by my side and that was it. I rolled my eyes before texting her back.

Sadie: I'm going over to Liam's house tonight.

Audrey: Oh. Did you want to cancel and maybe we could go out and get some drinks?

Sadie: No, I told you I have plans. Plans that I entered into willingly. Plans that I want. Nothing I would like to cancel on.

Audrey: Fine. Maybe tomorrow then?

Sadie: Maybe.

Audrey: Ok! I'll text you in the morning.

I'd never been the type of girl to blow her friends off for a guy, but lately, I didn't feel like Audrey has been much of a friend to me, constantly bringing up how she had such a weird feeling about Liam. I liked to think I was a pretty good judge of character though, and he'd been nothing but kind to me over the last few months.

I attached Daisy's leash to her collar, grabbed some chew toys for her and my pullover sweater and we were out our door, heading over to Liam's apartment. He said he was jumping in the shower, so he left the front door unlocked for us to come in. Stepping inside, it was warm and cozy and smelled like him—woodsy with a hint of fresh linen. I took my shoes off at the front door, removed Daisy's leash, and dropped my purse on a leather barstool.

Since we were together more often now, Liam wanted Daisy to feel just as at home at his place as she did at her own home, so he'd ordered her a plush dog bed. When he'd told me, my little heart leapt. As soon as she did a lap around the apartment, she made her way over to her bed and got comfortable. I knocked on the bathroom to let Liam know I was there.

I grabbed a large iced tea and got cozy up on the couch. When we stayed in, we had a very strict comfortable clothes only policy, so I was wearing my favorite leggings and an old college sweatshirt. Liam's iPad was sitting next to me on the couch, so I went to move it to the end table just to avoid any casualties. When I picked it up, the screen turned on and there were two text messages: one from me and the other from someone named Tommy—Liam had mentioned a bunch of his friends in passing, but I didn't recall him ever mentioning someone named Tommy L. I didn't think twice about it until a minute later, another text came in.

The shower water was still running, so I shifted to the other side of the couch where I had placed the device. I wasn't normally a nosey person, I chose to trust people until they proved that they were untrustworthy, but my radar wouldn't let me *not* look into this. I tapped the screen and read the two messages.

Tommy L: Joe, where are you?

Tommy L: Man, people are looking for you.

My pulse quickened and I panicked. Who was Tommy and who was he calling Joe? Was that Liam's middle name? Maybe a name close friends and family used? I knew all of the "red flags" that Audrey pointed out were most likely not real, so I took some deep breaths to calm myself down. Liam could read me like a book, so I needed to be as cool as a cucumber when he got out of the shower. I got myself back in check, attributing my skepticism to Audrey just getting in my head. I did, however, have full intentions of looking Tommy up tonight when I got home to see if I could find him anywhere online.

I was long back on my side of the couch and reading a book I had left here when Liam came out of the bathroom.

"Hello, beautiful," At this I looked up, Liam only had a towel draped around his waist.

"Hey! Did you want me to get started on dinner while you get changed?" I asked, secretly hoping he would say no because I was too cozy.

"No, why don't we just order some take-out and have it delivered? I know we planned on cooking, but pizza sounds just a little bit better. And besides, you look really comfortable and I don't want you to have to move."

I smiled, I did have a craving for some pizza. "I am fully onboard with that idea."

"Good, now get back to your book." Liam went back into the bedroom to get changed, and from my spot on the couch, I could see the whole process (which was certainly a nice view), but he didn't see me glance up from my book when he checked his phone. Assuming that he was looking at the messages from Tommy, I watched as his brows furrowed, his lips pulled together in a tight line, and his jaw was rigid. Liam clearly had some issues with this guy because he typed back aggressively before slamming his phone down on his bed.

I looked back down at my book, I had never seen Liam frustrated and mad like that before. Instead of asking about it, I chose to leave it alone. If Liam wanted to tell me about it, then he would in his own time.

For the rest of the night, Liam acted like nothing was wrong. Maybe I was just overthinking it; what if Tommy was just a co-worker who was asking where he was? That didn't explain the Joe part of it, but it was a reasonable explanation.

CHAPTER 23

Liam

I KNEW SADIE SAW ME THROW MY PHONE ON THE BED. That was what happened when your past crept into your present. I had full intentions of telling Sadie the truth, but I needed some more time for things to blow over before I told her everything.

Sadie called Delmonico's and ordered our pizzas. I left my phone in the bedroom on the charger, I didn't want any more messages from Tommy ruining my evening with Sadie. She'd had a long week and it was only Wednesday, so tonight was definitely not the night to tell her all about my past and the baggage that came with it. I felt bad, she'd been completely honest with me and she knew a solid fifteen percent about me. The lies I'd come up with had been pretty convincing, hell, *I* even started to believe them.

With Hailey's body washing ashore, I knew there would be some questions I would have to answer . . . ones that would land me on trial. I promised myself that I would do my best not to raise any red flags with Sadie, but with Tommy texting me, he was blowing my cover and making that more difficult.

CHAPTER 24

Sadie

Last night was uneventful. Liam and I ate pizza and put on movies as background noise while we read. Not one of our more fun nights of sitting and talking for hours, but he seemed a little bit off, so I just left it alone. He probably had a bad day at work and was still cranky from it, which explained the texts from Tommy if they were looking for him to log back on or something.

I had searched for Tommy L. on all social media channels this morning, but did you even know how many of them there were in the United States alone? A lot. And not knowing where this guy lived, I was fresh out of luck. At this point, I chose to put my trust in Liam and figured he would tell me when the time was right and he was ready to talk about it.

I texted Liam first thing this morning to say good morning and to thank him for paying for the pizza last night, but now it was noon and still no response. I didn't read into it, some days he was busier while working than others. He used to work whatever hours he wanted (mainly in the evenings), but now that we were together, he kept the same 9-to-5 hours that I did so we could spend time together.

I finished up my last design around four and called it a day. I was pretty productive and only had a few inquiry emails I needed to get back to, but I saved those for Friday mornings. There was no better way to kick off the weekend than by chatting with prospective clients and potentially bringing in new business.

Audrey had texted me this morning to see if I wanted to get dinner tonight. At first I was hesitant, but I knew she probably wanted to apologize, and I knew I should as well. It would be good for us both to go.

Right on time, both Audrey and I pulled up to the Chinese restaurant. She parked next to me, so I looked over and she waved, a small smile on her lips.

"Hey," I called over to her quietly.

She walked over and wrapped me in a hug, very un-Audrey-like. "Hey, I've missed you."

It had been the longest we'd ever gone without talking to or seeing each other. "I've missed you, too."

We walked in and were immediately seated. We wasted no time on ordering our food, we were both starving. I'd be lying if I said that it wasn't awkward, and it was evident that neither of us knew how to broach the apology. Finally getting sick of the silence, I broke it.

"So, what have you been up to?"

Her eyes darted down, something was wrong. "Nothing much, work has been a little bit busier than usual because they're releasing some new software, but other than that, it's been quiet. Mom and dad are getting ready to move."

I nodded, that was the end of my questions. I awkwardly swished around the ice in my water glass to pass the time.

"What have you been up to?" A few minutes had passed before she broke the silence.

"Not a whole lot. Liam and I have been hanging out more—almost every night—and he bought a bed for Daisy for his place for when we're over." A smile played on my lips. "Aside from that, work has been good, I'm fully booked."

"Sadie, that's fantastic! I'm so proud of you!"

Apparently talking about work did the trick because I could see her shoulders visibly relax. The rest of the dinner was really nice, we talked about everything except Liam and what happened between Audrey and I last Monday at dinner. It felt like there was an unspoken apology on both sides and we were going to move on.

I tried to be present at dinner and not on my phone, so as soon as I got in the car, I checked it to see if Liam had answered me yet. It had been about twelve hours and still no word from him. I made the executive decision to knock on his door when I got home to see if he was okay.

I pulled into my garage, went to let Daisy out in the yard, then walked over to Liam's to see if he was home. I rang the bell and waited a few minutes—no answer. Even though the snow was long gone and the May air was warmer, I still didn't want to be waiting outside for no reason. I went back home and waited to see if I got a text message, but by the time I went to bed, I still hadn't heard from him. Now I was concerned.

CHAPTER 25

Audrey

WHEN I GOT HOME FROM DINNER, I WAS STILL SHAKEN. This morning's events were still fresh in my mind. I knew Sadie and I were on good terms again, but how did I tell her that her boyfriend came over to my house today and threatened me? I sat down on the couch and closed my eyes, feeling myself getting dragged back into the flashback.

There'd been a knock on my door, which was weird, because I hadn't been expecting anyone. I'd looked out the peephole and saw Joe standing there, causing my pulse to quicken and my body to break out in a cold sweat. I wiped my hands on my jeans, plastered a fake smile on my face, and opened the door.

"Hey, Liam, how are you?"

"May I come in?" There was no hello, he meant business.

"Yes, of course!" We walked into the kitchen, thankfully my laptop and notebook were put away in my bedroom. "Can I get you something to drink?"

"No, you know why I'm here." His normally green eyes had taken on a deeper tone, almost making them look black. The tone of his voice was icy.

"I . . . don't, I'm sorry. Is this about Sadie?"

"No, and you know that. Stop playing this game, Audrey."

"Liam, I really don't know what you're talking about . . ." I knew exactly what he was talking about. How did he know that I was looking into him?

His voice went up an octave when he said, "How about you stop playing the dumb, innocent card for one fucking second and just be honest. Did you tell Sadie?"

I knew I had to be honest, if for no other reason, to protect Sadie. "No, I didn't."

"Well, that's a damn surprise. You've not liked me from the minute we met—now, why is that?"

"Something in my gut told me that you weren't a good person. I don't know what Sadie sees in you."

"She trusts very easily. That's something that could get her killed you know. I'm just here to tell you to stop looking into me before things end very badly for you, Audrey."

"Are you threatening me?" I already knew the answer to that. "How did you know that I was looking into you?"

"The only thing I haven't lied to Sadie about is working in computer software, that was my last job as Joe Hale. Before I left, I set up an alert when someone looked into Liam Reynolds or Joe Hale. Normally, I just leave things alone because I don't know the people and they don't know me personally. Imagine my surprise when I saw that an IP address in Red Oak was looking into me."

I swallowed hard, not sure what to say to any of that. I had to ask a question that I didn't want to know the answer to. "The other day when I came back from my walk and all my browser tabs were closed . . . was, was that you?"

"Yes, it was." This guy never seems to blink, that was possibly the creepiest part about him. "So, I'm going to leave now. You *won't* be telling Sadie about any of this."

Just like that, Joe was out of my house once again.

Now that I was threatened, I couldn't tell Sadie. I just had to go along with everything she said; feigning happiness and pretending that everything she was telling me about "Liam" was just the most fascinating thing I had ever heard. Not only did I now have to keep this massive secret, but I was also in danger. I had to figure out a way to keep Sadie safe as best as I could which meant I wouldn't be able to tell her right away.

CHAPTER 26

Sadie

I T WAS AN EARLY-MAY MORNING AND THE SUN WAS already blinding through the curtains. Seeing that the sun was shining made getting up and out of bed easier than normal. I had forgotten my phone in the living room last night and didn't need it for my alarm since it was a Friday, and Fridays were my "no alarm" days. I grabbed a lightweight sweatshirt and threw that on over my T-shirt and pajama shorts, making my way over to Daisy's bed to give her some pets while she was still asleep. That was one reason I knew she was meant to be my dog: she slept in and got up only when she was ready. She lived her life on her own schedule.

I shuffled to the kitchen to make myself an iced caramel macchiato; as soon as May rolled around, I break out the iced drinks. While my espresso was brewing, I grabbed my phone off the charger. Not having my phone right next to me all night seemed to help me wake up in a better mood . . . until I remembered that Liam hadn't talked with me at all yesterday. I scrolled through my notifications, giving priority to the text messages: one from my cousin, one from a client, and one from Liam from an hour ago. I clicked on that one first.

> Liam: Hey, I'm so sorry I didn't message you back at all yesterday. My dad called early in the morning and told me that he wasn't doing so well and needed some help and wanted some company. I was there until the early hours this morning, so I'm going to get some sleep and should be up by noon. Talk to you then!

> Sadie: Good morning! I'm so sorry to hear that, is he doing better now? Let me know when you're up, I was planning on going for a lunchtime walk and would love some company.

I knew he was probably asleep, so I went about my morning. I had my potential client calls and they went very well, so I was starting the weekend off on the right foot. Right around 11:30, my phone buzzed from its spot on my desk, it was from Liam.

> Liam: A walk now would be awesome. I was inside most of yesterday, so I could use a little fresh air with my favorite girls.

> Sadie: I just need to put my shoes on and I'll be ready to go. Meet outside in five minutes?

I slipped on my tennis shoes, put Daisy's leash on, grabbed a water bottle and portable dog bowl, and we were ready to go on a nice, long walk. When I walked outside and pushed my sunglasses up on my nose, Liam was right there as well. What a contrast to when he stood me up for drinks. We walked hand-in-hand around the neighborhood, then strolled around the greenway that was nearby while we talked about his dad and how he was doing, then we pivoted to my client calls from this morning.

When we stopped to give Daisy some water, Liam and I sat on a bench to rest. I took a moment to appreciate my life—surely there was no way that it could ever get better than this. Well, except if I could figure out what to do with the camera-filled book . . .

LATE SUMMER

CHAPTER 27

Audrey

SADIE MENTIONED THE OTHER DAY THAT SHE AND JOE were leaving for a weekend getaway and I didn't feel comfortable with this at all. For two months now, I'd had confirmation that Liam was in fact Joe and I hadn't said a word to Sadie. I knew people would judge me if they knew that, but he didn't specifically threaten her. I was operating under the assumption that he had the potential to be dangerous, so I was trying my best to keep my mouth shut. I obviously had my own suspicions, but Joe had been interrogated multiple times when he lived in Tampa after Hailey's disappearance and each time he passed the lie detector test, so the police ruled him out as a person of interest.

From everything Sadie had told me since March, Joe seemed to be treating her very well and she didn't have any concerns. And if after five months she still wasn't concerned, then I'd try my best to just silence the alarm and let her live her life . . . no matter how hard it was for me. I'd had to stop talking with her every day because hearing her talk about him constantly and what they were doing just made me nauseous. Maybe he was planning on telling Sadie about Hailey in his own time.

The fact that the two of them were set to be in a secluded cabin in the middle of the woods just doesn't sit well, though. I didn't have verification that he killed his ex-girlfriend, but all arrows were pointing back to him. It was far too coincidental that he moved as soon as her body was found; seemed like a guilty conscience and running away to me.

I dove further into Hailey's case, starting from the beginning to see if I could put any more pieces together, but no luck. After all these years, the police were coming up empty—no luck finding any evidence. After six months of heavy investigation, it sounded like the detectives had filed it as a cold case, which outraged her family. From what I'd read, everyone loved Hailey, they couldn't think of anyone who would want to hurt her.

I was on the third page of Google results when I stumbled upon a blog post that was published just after Joe moved here; it was someone's take on why Joe Hale was the one who had the motive to kill her. I looked at the name, Kelly Moran. *Where have I heard that name before?* I thought about it for a minute, realizing that was the same Kelly Moran whose profile I used to help me find Hailey's.

Let me start off by saying that Hailey was one of my very best friends, we were glued at the hip. We went through school together, dated guys that were friends, and had regular Wednesday night ladies' nights. She was one of the only people who I would trust with my life. I can't believe she was missing for so many years. When her Instagram profile was still being updated, I had held out hope that she would be found alive.

Even though Joe was the one who called the police to report Hailey missing, I thought it was more suspicious because I knew the truth.

I knew that Hailey wasn't happy in her relationship with Joe, she'd wanted to end things. I knew that she had once cheated on him with one of our other friends. Joe had found out and was furious at first, but then told her that they could work out their differences; that was two weeks before Hailey went missing. If you ask me, that's all the motive someone as controlling as Joe needed. I've told the police this multiple times over the last few years, but they never believed me because I had no way to prove my allegations. Until I did.

Once Hailey's Instagram account was being updated again, I showed the police that the captions were written completely differently than how Hailey used to. There were no exclamation points, no emojis, no lack of punctuation at the end of the caption. I knew this meant someone had her account logged into their phone. I also knew that it meant that someone had access to all of Hailey's pictures, because some of the ones that were being shared were older. No matter what I showed them, they didn't seem to believe that it was enough to arrest a man who was doing a very good job of putting on an air that he was just distraught, even leading the search for her. It's sick if you ask me.

Now that my best friend's body has washed ashore, it confirmed what I believed all those years ago: Joe killed her and dumped her body somewhere. Now, instead of staying here and mourning like the rest of us, demanding answers, he just up and left. Does that not scream guilty to anyone else?

Hailey was such a beautiful, bright light in our community and her death has left a massive hole in it. I hope she knew how immensely she was loved and how deeply she is missed. If you know anything at all, please reach out to the Tampa Police Department.

My mouth hung open, did this girl just confirm everything I had thought? Every ounce of my being wanted to send her a message and ask if she had some time to talk. Screw it, now my best friend could be in danger and I wanted to know how to prevent this from happening. I opened Facebook and typed out a message explaining who I was and why I was reaching out to her, I hesitated, but then pressed send.

It didn't take long for her to respond, and when she did, she sent me her phone number and told me to give her a call. I dialed the number while my knee bounced, unsure of what I was going to learn during this call.

"Hello?" a sweet voice asked, answering my call.

"Hi, is this Kelly?" My knee bounced faster.

"It is, is this Audrey?"

"Yeah. Thank you for taking the time to talk with me, I think that I might have a similar situation on my hands to yours. I just read your blog. My friend Sadie is dating Joe."

"You know where Joe is?"

"He's up here in Vermont, he's going by the name of Liam Reynolds."

There was silence on the other end of the phone. "How did you put two and two together?"

"When I met him, he gave off a weird vibe, so I started looking into him. So I took her through all my amateur detective work. I wasn't about to divulge that I used her profiles to find Joe.

"Yeah, I understand what you're saying. I had a similar feeling when I first met him, but then he seemed normal, so I just didn't think anything else of it."

We chatted for a while, she shared some sweet anecdotes about Hailey and their friendship and all I could think about was Sadie. What could I possibly do to help her get out of this situation? I couldn't bring it up because I knew she wouldn't believe me, I just needed to plant seeds of doubt in her.

CHAPTER 28

Sadie

LIAM AND I WERE LEAVING FOR OUR FIRST COUPLE'S getaway this morning. We both agreed that we wanted to get away for the weekend, so we found a cabin on the lake and rented it for two nights. The cabin didn't allow pets, so last night I dropped Daisy off with Audrey. There were restaurants around, but we planned on cooking most of our meals. We enjoyed the occasional meal out when we were home, but Liam definitely preferred to spend the nights at home. Which I didn't mind, but it was beginning to feel like he didn't want to be seen in public with me.

We both took today off from work to get a head start on our weekend. It was a four-hour drive, so we left around eight to beat traffic. The first stop on our list was Starbucks; once the coffee was acquired, we put the top back and our windows down and enjoyed the beautiful August morning. The glowing sun was warm against my skin, it felt like years since it had last embraced me.

We rode in silence for the first part of the drive, but once we got back in the car after our bathroom break, we put some music on and actually relaxed. I knew that the only thing we were both thinking about was that this would be the first time we'd be sleeping together. Let me rephrase that. We'd *slept* together, but we hadn't ever stayed the night together. This would be our first official sleepover. Liam was really great about all this—he respected that I wanted to take things relatively slowly. It sounded so strange, but sleeping in bed with someone just seemed so personal and intimate. Probably because it was when you were the most vulnerable.

With only thirty minutes left in the drive, we had to stop for gas. So, while Liam filled up the tank, I went inside to grab some snacks: gummy worms, Hershey's chocolate bars, M&M's, and chips . . . road trip essentials. In ten minutes flat, we were back on the road. We pulled off onto a dirt road, and a dust cloud enveloped the car.

"I think it's right up here on the left." Liam pointed ahead to a small wood cabin.

As the dust cleared and the most adorable little house came into view. It was set right out on the water overlooking the prettiest crystal clear blue lake I had ever seen. We pulled up to it and my mouth was slightly agape. It was even more quaint up close. There were some Adirondack chairs placed around a firepit right at the water's edge—that would make for a cozy night. We walked up a few wooden stairs and up to the door, I paused, inhaling deeply. The smell of the lake was intoxicating, like the smell of a new chapter. Using the passcode we were given, we were able to get right in.

The inside of the cabin was decorated to the nines. When you walked in, it was just one big space. The bedroom and bathroom were off to the left and the kitchen and living space were to the right. I went to the bedroom to put my suitcase down, the floors were carpeted with a cashmere-colored carpet. The wall to my left was a white and to the right was half white, half natural-colored wood that led up to the ceiling. There was a deer pelt under the light oak bed and a beautiful quilt on the bed; it was decorated as a modern cabin and I loved it. The wall that led out to the balcony overlooking the lake was painted a deep gray and had beautiful French doors. I walked into the living space and the floors were a light distressed oak color, the walls a pale gray. The kitchen consisted of grays and whites and fit the feel of the house perfectly.

Liam was in the kitchen, putting away the groceries we brought with us.

"It's beautiful, huh?" I asked, walking towards him, wrapping my arms around his torso.

He jumped at my touch, so I said, "Sorry, didn't mean to scare you!"

"You're good, I just zoned out. What did you say?"

"I said it's beautiful here, isn't it?"

"Yeah, it's lovely."

"What did you want to do this afternoon?" I was hoping for nothing so I could sit outside and read. I *was* a bookworm after all.

"Did you want to go for a swim?" he asked, eyebrow raised, smirk playing on his lips.

I thought about it, a solid second choice. "I'll go throw a suit on!" I started for the bedroom, but Liam was opening the refrigerator; he wanted lunch first.

"Go put your suit on, I'm going to make a sandwich. Want one?" His voice was muffled, his head still in the refrigerator while he dug through our groceries. I knew we brought too much, but I would rather have too much and have options, than not enough.

I playfully stroked my chin, pretending to think about it. "Can I have a turkey and cheese with mayo, please?"

"Coming right up."

I slipped out of my shorts and tank top and put on my blue and white floral print bikini. Since the weather warmed up, we'd been going on long walks either during lunch or after work. All I'd needed was a little bit of exercise and to not be so lonely (which stopped my boredom snacking) and this summer was the first one that I actually felt confident. I put a coverup over my bathing suit and went back to the kitchen with full intentions of annihilating that sandwich.

Standing next to Liam again, he was just putting the final touches on his ham and turkey sandwich. "Ready to eat?"

My stomach growled in response.

"I'll take that as a yes." He placed both plates down on the dining room table and we ate in silence, admiring the beautiful lake from our seats. I was so hungry, my sandwich lasted not even five minutes.

"Do you want another one?" Liam asked, only half-done with his.

"Nope, I'm full, I was just hungrier than I thought."

"Now we have to wait a half hour before going swimming," he teased, trying to get a rise out of me.

"That's such bullshit. You sound like my mom."

"Your mom is a smart woman, so I'll take that as a compliment." It had taken two months, but I finally felt comfortable having Liam meet my parents and grandparents. We went over for a Sunday dinner at my grandparents' house and I was so nervous that my insides felt like Jell-O. Liam brought flowers for my mom and grandma and everyone fell into a natural conversation that flowed nicely. That night, by the time we were ready to leave, Liam had made separate plans to see each of them again . . . without me. He felt comfortable enough to spend time with them all without me there—that was huge in my book. Even though we hadn't been dating very long, my mom, just last week, brought up a wedding and if that was an avenue I was considering. I knew I needed more time to fully sort out my feelings to see if they were long-term or not.

We finished up lunch and I filled the dishwasher while Liam

put on his swimsuit. He reappeared wearing a tank top and blue striped boardshorts—we didn't plan on it, but color-wise, we matched. We made our way down to the water; I placed my beach bag with towels and sunscreen on one of the Adirondack chairs and slipped out of my coverup.

"Wow . . ." Liam had his sunglasses on so I couldn't see what he was looking at, but he was looking in my general direction, so it was either me or the water behind me.

"Me?"

"Yes, you!"

A blush crept up my cheeks. "Thank you."

Wasting no time, I went for the water, not stopping until I was waist-deep. The water had a slight chill to it, but it was refreshing. Liam joined me and we swam for hours before my stomach started beckoning me for my attention again.

"I had a thought about tonight," Liam said, drying his hair off with a towel. "Why don't we go in and shower, then we can make some dinner and sit out here on the chairs and watch the sunset?"

I wrapped my arms around his toned stomach. "I think that sounds perfect."

"You can go in and get cleaned up first, I'll start getting everything out that we need for dinner."

I nodded and made my way back inside, trying to track as little water through the house as humanly possible. I took a quick shower and put on my pajamas—we had no plans of going anywhere and I wanted nothing more than to be comfortable. When I walked into the kitchen, Liam looked different than he did twenty minutes ago. He looked . . . annoyed? Agitated? I wasn't sure.

"Hey, the bathroom is all yours."

"Sounds good."

"You okay? Is something bothering you?"

I could see he tried to snap himself out of it. "Yeah, I'm sorry, something just came up with work. I have to be back early on Sunday. Would you mind if we left earlier than we planned?"

I winced, I didn't want to leave earlier, but it was for his job, so I couldn't say no. I tried to be understanding, but I couldn't shake the pang of sadness in my chest when I realized that this was how my relationship with Ben started to go downhill. Work started getting in the way.

"Yeah, of course. We'll make the best out of what time we do have. What time were you planning on?"

"Ideally, I'd like to be in the car by 6:00 a.m. if we can."

"Wow, that's way earlier than we were planning on . . ." I tried to hide the sadness in my voice.

"I know, and I'm really sorry. They just called and said that the software that they use has a bug in it and it needs to be fixed. I wrote the coding, so I'm the only one who can fix it."

"It's okay, we'll make the best of the time we have." I planted a kiss on his cheek.

"I'm going to go shower, why don't you take a book out on the balcony and relax? When I come out, we can start cooking."

I lunged for my book on the bed. "Don't have to tell me twice!" I headed out the French doors and planted myself at the little table that was out there. There was something about reading on vacation that just made everything feel right in the world. Maybe it was the warm breeze on my freshly showered skin or maybe it was the serene atmosphere, but diving into this book was easier than usual. The characters and the setting just came to life and I was easily lost in it, not noticing that Liam came out of the bathroom and sat down at the table with me.

"Whatcha reading?"

I snapped back to reality. "Just a cheesy romance, nothing super exciting."

"Is it as cheesy as our love story?"

"Hmm . . . maybe just a little bit cheesier." A wide grin spread across my face, I was really thankful to be here with Liam and enjoying the beautiful summer weather. I seemed to thrive during the summer and early fall. The rest of the year was miserable for me with how cold it was and with my allergies.

Liam looked down at his phone, checking the time. "Did you want to start making dinner? By the time we're done, the sun should be getting ready to set."

"Yeah, that sounds good. We can eat out by the water, it'll be pretty."

We headed to the kitchen, I was running point on the sides, so I opened the bag of fries and put them on a baking sheet before cutting up the onions, lettuce, and tomatoes for our burgers. While Liam grilled up some hamburgers and toasted the buns, I made the arugula salad we had planned. It was nice to act as the sous chef for once; I planned on letting Liam do the bulk of the cooking this weekend.

We assembled our plates and made our way down to the water's edge, plopping down in the Adirondack chairs, just as the sun started to dip in the sky.

"Shouldn't be long now." Liam motioned over to the sunset that was forming.

By the time my burger was gone, the sunset was in full-swing and it was the most beautiful thing I had ever seen. The blue sky was painted with pinks, oranges, and yellows, and it formed the prettiest reflection on the water. Being in Vermont might suck in the winters, but damn, there were some gorgeous summer sunsets. Once the sky turned dark blue and the moon rose in the sky, it was our cue to go back inside—the mosquitoes were starting to bite and while I was normally extraordinarily prepared, I somehow forgot bug spray.

We cleaned up our plates and made ourselves comfortable on the couch, turning on the television. I grabbed the blanket I brought and snuggled up into Liam's side.

"This is nice, isn't it?" I spoke up after a few minutes of the movie we were watching.

"Yeah, it is. I couldn't pick a better person to come here with, too. I wish we could stay longer, though."

"Well, we still have all day tomorrow to enjoy. Let's not rush it." I planted a kiss on his lips.

CHAPTER 29

Liam

I WOKE UP BEFORE SADIE AND THE WAY THE MORNING SUN hit her face, it made her look even more beautiful—it hit her cheekbones in just the right way. This was the one time I could get away with staring at her, so I was taking full advantage.

Last night was the first time we actually slept together and I was surprised, it wasn't as uncomfortable as I thought it was going to be. When we lay down, Sadie cuddled up to me and her head fit perfectly in the crook of my neck. The last time I slept in the same bed with someone was Hailey and that was years ago. I wasn't sure how it would feel to be this vulnerable with someone again. If we were honest, it was weird to basically be comatose next to someone for eight hours at a time.

Sadie must have been able to feel that I was staring, because a few minutes later, her big blue eyes slowly started to open, still foggy with sleep.

"Good morning, sunshine." I placed a kiss on her exposed shoulder.

"Hi." Her voice was thick with sleep. "I need a few more minutes. What time is it?"

I looked down at my phone and told her, "Just after nine."

"Ugh." Sadie pulled the covers over her head, "I guess I should get up then."

"We're on vacation, you can sleep in as late as you'd like. No one will kick you out of this bed."

Her eyes closed. "What did you want to do today?"

"I was thinking maybe we could go on a small hike? I read that there are some waterfalls not too far from here. Looks like it's just over a mile."

Her eyes shot open. "I didn't bring the right footwear."

"Nice lie, I saw tennis shoes in your bag."

She rolled her eyes playfully. "Dang it, you caught me."

"I know hiking isn't your thing, but I promise, the waterfalls don't look real they're so pretty."

"Fine, as long as it's not far."

"It's not, I promise. Did you want to make breakfast?"

"I think I ate too many French fries last night, so I'm still good. You?"

"I had too many burgers." I laughed. "Once we get up and ready, we can go."

We both got out of bed and got changed into shorts and T-shirts, wearing our bathing suits underneath. As much as I knew Sadie wasn't thrilled about going on this hike, it meant the world to me that she was willing to go with me. While she was tying her shoe, I caught a glimpse of her face and could see something was up.

"You okay?"

"Yeah, why?"

"You just seem anxious," I observed.

She finished the knot and stood up. "I am, but it's all good. I'm just clumsy, so this isn't the safest activity for me."

"I'll be right there with you," I said, taking her head in my hands, "and I promise, this will be easy and worth it."

Sadie nodded, I could see some of her fears melting away.

I hadn't been lying to her, it really was only a little over two miles to the waterfalls and it was mostly flat. Sadie only grabbed my arm once when we were walking across some larger rocks.

"You doing okay?" I wanted to check-in on her since she was pretty quiet.

"Yeah, this isn't bad at all! I've just been focused on not losing my footing."

"Do you need to stop?"

"No, I'm good. I can see the falls in the distance!" She pointed to the right of us.

We walked another third of a mile and we were at the top of the most beautiful waterfall I had ever seen. It wasn't tall at all, but the way the water reflected the rays of sun, it was inviting.

We dropped our backpacks and slipped off our clothes, locking hands as we stepped on the edge of the waterfall. "Did you want to jump?"

"Hell yes I do!"

"I thought you were a scaredy cat?" I teased.

"Not scared of jumping off a cliff, more just scared of the inevitability of me tripping on a rock."

"I feel like you have your fears mixed up." A smile played on my lips, I was so thankful to be here with her.

Sadie stuck her tongue out at me, "Ready to jump?"

"I'll jump off any cliff with you."

I counted to three and we jumped, both hitting the water at the same time. I popped right back up, but Sadie was nowhere in sight.

"Sadie!" No response.

Panic set in. "Sadie! Sadie?"

I felt something grab my foot and yank me below the surface. I had enough time to take a deep breath, prepping for what might happen. As soon as my head was submerged, whatever was holding my ankle let go and I was able to swim back to the surface. This time, Sadie was there.

"Thank goodness you're alright!" I swam over to her, squeezing her tightly.

She was belly laughing. "I'm a good swimmer. Sorry if I scared you."

"As long as you're okay, that's all I care about."

She placed a wet kiss on my lips. "I'm just fine. I was thinking . . . maybe since we have to cut our weekend short, we could go out for dinner tonight?"

"I think that's a great idea. We can swim here for a bit, then we can go ahead and head on back. Do you have someplace in mind?"

"I was thinking Italian. There's a place called Indaco that's supposed to be really highly rated and it's only a half hour from here."

"Perfect. We can make a reservation when we get back to the cabin."

We were able to snag a seven o'clock reservation at Indaco and it was nice to put on some fancier clothes for once. Over the last few years, I'd lived in shorts and T-shirts, so having to wear khaki pants and a button-down shirt made me feel out of my element, but in a good way. I got ready first, giving Sadie the bedroom and bathroom while I waited on the couch, book in-hand.

"How come you never scroll on your phone like a normal person?" Sadie asked, standing in front of me wearing a pink and white long floral dress and white sandals. She looked stunning.

Her hair was down and in loose curls and the gold jewelry she was wearing complemented her newly sun-kissed skin perfectly.

"I don't have any social media accounts, that's why I don't scroll." I caught myself, I did have the Instagram account that I created when I moved to Vermont, but that was it. I hoped that she wouldn't ask any further questions about it. She accepted that answer and we were on our way to the restaurant. We sat in silence, I had run out of conversation topics for the weekend already, not a good sign. Sadie had definitely picked up on the lack of topics because she was sitting to my right, fidgeting with her hands.

"Hey, can I ask you a question?" She finally spoke up as we pulled up to a red stoplight.

"Of course, anything."

"I know you only have an Instagram account, but why don't you have anything else?" Oh, her questions were just delayed.

"I started the account when I moved here, but got bored with it. I've just never been a social media type of guy. The way I was raised, I was always outside, living in the moment, I never wanted to be chained behind a phone. And to be honest with you, I just don't care all that much about what other people are doing or what they think of me."

"I get that. I tried for a while to resist creating accounts on all social media platforms, but when you start your own business, you have to market yourself somehow." Sadie shrugged, an exasperated sigh escaped her lips.

"Sometimes it's all bad and there's no good to it." I was all too familiar with how social media could destroy someone's life.

She reached for my hand over the console. We pulled into the parking lot and made our way into the restaurant. For being in the more rural part of Vermont, this restaurant was surprisingly fancy. We were seated immediately and had already studied the menu, so we placed our order quickly. When the warm loaf of Italian bread was placed down on our table, we dove in like we had never seen food before—then I remembered we skipped both breakfast and lunch today.

"So, can I ask a follow-up question from our conversation earlier?"

"Absolutely." My pulse quickened, we *cannot* keep talking about me.

"Who's that Hailey girl you follow? I'm not jealous or anything, but is she a cousin or old co-worker?"

I inhaled sharply, this is exactly the conversation I was hoping to avoid. "She's an old friend. The only one I still keep in contact with from Florida."

"Where's Tommy from?"

My eyes widened. "Tommy who?"

I tried to play it off, I don't know how successful I was.

"Tommy L. I don't know, I saw his name pop up on your iPad a while ago."

"Oh, he's just someone I worked with." Did she read the messages or just see who they were from. If she didn't ask any more questions, then I knew we were good . . .

CHAPTER 30

Sadie

I KNEW I WAS PUSHING THE ENVELOPE BY ASKING ABOUT BOTH Hailey and Tommy. Both times, Liam gave me very short, generic answers and then shut the conversation down, not wanting to talk about it. For a brief second, I debated texting Audrey to see if she would look into Hailey, but thought better of it. I knew if I texted her, she would start to think that I was having doubts and then go into overdrive with her research. I'd just look into it when we get home tomorrow.

Our food came and it was delicious; I ordered eggplant parmigiana and Liam ordered chicken parmigiana—both came with more pasta than I had ever seen in my life, not that I was complaining. The conversation was flowing freely again; we talked about potential trips we could take in the fall, and how excited Daisy would be when I got home tomorrow. I didn't text Audrey to tell her that we were going to be home early, I figured I would still go over at dinner. It would give me some time to get the house tidied up and the laundry in the washing machine, while also enjoying a little "me time."

We asked for some to-go boxes while Liam paid, before heading to a cocktail bar that was just down the street from the restaurant. We had a drink there before making the drive back to the cabin.

As we sat on the couch in comfortable clothes, watching another movie, I looked over at Liam and he looked like he was everywhere but present.

"I'm still so full, but that food was so good, I want to eat some of the leftovers." I patted my stomach, trying to start up a conversation.

He stared blankly at the television.

"Liam?"

Still nothing, so I tried again. "Liam?"

He shook his head, snapping out of his daze. "Yeah?"

"Nothing, I just said that I was still full and the food was delicious."

"Oh."

Clearly he was not in the mood to talk again.

Liam's alarm clock was blaring at 4:30 this morning, an absolutely awful time to get up and start your day. I threw a bra on and stayed in my pajamas for the car ride; I wasn't about to put real clothes on this early in the morning. We packed our suitcases last night, so all we had to do this morning was put them in the trunk and put the groceries we brought in the cooler. Liam took care of that while I attempted to keep my eyes open until we were on the road, which was futile. As soon as my seatbelt was buckled, I was asleep again. I woke up around seven, two hours into our drive, just as the sun was starting to poke above the trees.

"Do you need to stop?" Liam asked quietly.

"I could probably use some coffee soon." I was wiping the sleep out of my eyes.

"You and me both. I'm not looking forward to working as soon as we get home."

"I'm sorry that you have to, I'm sure they appreciate the fact that you're working on a Sunday."

"Yeah, I really hope they do, too." While it made sense in the context of our conversation, his response seemed too loaded.

We pulled into a Starbucks and got two large hot coffees to breathe life back into our bodies since we were out later than expected. I fell asleep sometime around one and I didn't know when Liam did. All I knew was that three and a half hours of sleep wasn't enough for my late-twentysomething self anymore.

Now that I had a coffee, I was better able to keep Liam company for the rest of the trip. The remainder of the drive flew by and was really relaxing, a nice way to ease back into reality.

We pulled into his driveway just around ten and I subconsciously breathed a sigh of relief. I wasn't sure why, but I'd felt kind of uptight this weekend, though they were probably just nerves.

He carried my bag to my door for me. And when he placed his hands on my hips lightly, he said, "I had a really great time with you this weekend, Sadie. I'm going to head home and get to work. I'll talk to you later, okay?"

I stood on my toes, moving closer to his lips. "I'm going to go back to bed." I planted a sleepy kiss on his lips and went to open my door, but it was already unlocked. My stomach fell to my feet, someone had been in my house.

CHAPTER 31

Audrey

MY PHONE WAS RINGING. NO ONE CALLED ME THIS EARLY, especially on a Sunday morning. I flipped it over to be met with Sadie's face. My stomach sank.

"Hello?"

"Audrey, can you come over? Someone broke into my house and the police are on their way."

"I'll be right there. Stay outside," I told her, pulse quickening.

I threw on some clothes and sped over to Sadie's house, making it there just after the police arrived. Sadie was on the lawn with Detective Landry. When your town is as small as ours, you recognize the local law enforcement. I walked over to them as Liam was walking away. I gave Sadie a side hug and asked her where Liam was going.

"He has to go get some work done. That's why I called you to help keep me calm. Someone was in my house. They're pulling the security footage now, so hopefully that picked something up."

My heart broke for her, what a scary thing to come home to. "Everything will be alright, okay?"

Her hands were shaking. "Yeah, I hope so. Is Daisy okay?"

"She was the perfect houseguest." A small smile crept up Sadie's lips.

"Sadie, the house is clear; you're safe to go in," Detective Landry told her.

She looked at me warily. "Can you come in with me?"

"Of course, I'll stay with you."

I stayed with Sadie all afternoon while she waited patiently for Liam to be done with his work so he could come stay with her tonight. As the afternoon went on, I needed to leave to go let Daisy out, so Sadie had to stay alone, which, she was not happy about. I didn't blame her, though.

While I was gone, Detective Landry went back over to get some more information from Sadie. When I got back to her around six, Daisy in tow, she told me that Liam said he wasn't able to come back tonight, the problem at work was worse than they had thought and it might take a few days. *I could scream at how sick and tired I am of having to call him Liam when I know every bit of real information,* I thought bitterly. I managed to keep it together pretty well, only getting annoyed with her around nine when she was telling how nice it felt to sleep next to someone again.

It's getting harder and harder for me to keep this massive secret to myself. I just found it beyond coincidental that in the three years that Sadie had lived there, nothing had ever been a concern, but now, all of a sudden, she went out of town and her house got broken into. Maybe it *was* just a coincidence and I was thinking too much into it, but I didn't believe it.

CHAPTER 32

Liam

I can't believe that someone would break into Sadie's house. Just seeing the pure fear on her face when she realized what happened was heartbreaking. I imagine that having your house broken into has to be the ultimate invasion of privacy. I wish I could have stayed with her, but I'd needed to take care of some things. My first order of business was figuring out why Tommy was reaching out to me again and how he got my new phone number.

I had dumped my suitcase from the weekend out on my bed and threw in enough clothes for a few days. I needed some time in Florida to tie up some loose ends and see my friends—well, those who would actually want to see me, anyway. I texted Tommy back and told him what time my flight landed tonight and that I would need a ride. He obliged, and I managed to leave my house without Sadie knowing; she needed to think that I was home all week, just "working." I waited for Audrey to leave so I knew no one would be on lookout and walked down the street to another house and had an Uber pick me up there and drop me off at Burlington International Airport. All of this felt sneaky, but I knew that it was what I needed to do in order to keep my past at bay and keep my eye on the prize.

I was through security in no time, keeping my carry-on with me—it made it quicker to get out of the airport on the other side. I grabbed a sandwich and a bottle of water at the convenience store and sat at my gate, filling my stomach for the first time today. I stared out the window, waiting for my boarding class to be called. I only sat there for ten minutes before it was my turn to board the plane. I sat down in my first-class seat and put my headphones in, tuning out the world.

At some point before take off, I must fallen asleep, because now we were halfway through our trek and landing in New Jersey. We had an hour-long layover before we boarded yet another plane and landed in Tampa. I was thankful for short flights because I hated flying; it was my biggest fear in life . . . well, that and being convicted of a murder.

We disembarked the plane and I made my way to the arrivals area, waiting for Tommy. I checked my texts once more, confirming that this was where he said he would be. I waited twenty minutes, ready to call an Uber, but eventually a black Jeep pulled up. I would recognize that Jeep anywhere. The number of summer nights I spent riding around Tampa, the roof and doors off, was countless. I smiled inwardly, it was nice to feel like I was home again, even though I hadn't been gone all that long. The hot, humid air made me regret not bringing a swimsuit, but I could run to the store if I really wanted to.

I took a deep breath and opened the back door, putting my suitcase on the seat, then hopped in the passenger side.

"It's good to see you again. What name are you going by now, Joey?" Tommy's voice was still just as gruff as when I left.

"Liam Reynolds."

"Damn, dude, that sounds pretentious. You couldn't come up with something a little better than that? I mean, if you're going to reinvent yourself, wouldn't you go for something a little cooler?"

"Shut up, man. Why am I even here?" A smile spread across my face, Tommy had been my best friend for years, I hated moving and not giving him my new phone number to keep in contact.

"We have to talk." We had an unconventional relationship; we'd been friends for eight years, then I started dating his sister, Hailey, three years later. Even though Hailey and I were pretty serious, it never changed the relationship I had with Tommy—if anything, it made us feel even closer as friends because I was almost family . . . until Hailey went missing.

That was the day I died inside. She was my best friend, I thought we were going to grow old together. I was planning on asking her to marry me the weekend she went missing. But, instead, my heart was ripped out. When I called her disappearance in, everyone immediately thought it was me. I understood—the first suspect was always the spouse, but I had no motive for hurting her. Why would I want to hurt someone I loved so incredibly much?

I stayed in Tampa until earlier this year, when Hailey's body was finally found on that beach. During those three long years, people eventually stopped believing it was me and just went on with their lives. How I wish I could have done the same. When her body was found, it put everyone's eyes back on me and it got to be too much. This time I had the resources to get out of here, so I packed up and disappeared under the cloak of darkness. I told Tommy that I was going to Vermont, but didn't give him my new name or any contact information.

We pulled up to his house, a place I hadn't lived for the last six months, and I stared at it for a moment. I had so many good memories in those four walls, I didn't know what he could possibly need to talk with me about. I grabbed my bag and we went inside—it looked exactly as I last saw it. The walls were still a dark gray, the hole in the wall that I punched when Hailey went missing was still there, the one kitchen cabinet falling off the wall. This was my home, this was where I belonged.

Tommy sat down on the couch and I followed suit. "So, what's this about?" I asked.

"They think they found the guy that killed Hailey, but the police wanted to talk to you one more time." Tommy paused, giving me a moment to process what he had just said. "I know talking with them again is the last thing that you want to do, but I promise, this could actually bring us the closure we've been waiting three years for."

"Who was it?" was all I was able to get out through gritted teeth.

"They haven't told us any further information yet, they wanted to talk with you first."

A pit formed in my stomach, but I said, "Okay."

I slept like shit last night. Tommy was right, the last thing I wanted to do was spend my morning at the Tampa Police Department, but here I was, once again trying to clear my name and help them catch the guy who killed Hailey. I had to keep reminding myself: this was all for Hailey.

Detective Sanders sat down in front of me. His auburn hair a little longer and more gray than the last time I saw him when we were doing the initial interrogation three years ago.

"Hello again, Joseph."

"Detective Sanders," I nodded.

He sat down, "How have you been? It's been a bit since we've seen ya around here."

"I've been good. After everything that happened with Hailey, I needed to get away for a bit."

"And change your name, too, I hear."

"That's correct."

"Why did you do that, Joe?"

I looked at him in the eye. "So that if anyone had heard of me before, they wouldn't recognize my new name. I wanted a fresh start. I *deserve* a fresh start. She was the love of my life and I lost her. I think a lot of people had forgotten that."

That answer seemed to shut him up. "Can you tell me the details again of when you noticed Hailey was missing?"

I recounted the story for what felt like the two hundredth time. I told him how I hadn't heard from her in twenty-four hours and that was when I'd called the police. Yes, I knew it was soon, but it wasn't normal for us. I led the search party, I hung the fliers, I did everything I could to find her. I wasn't the suspect they were looking for.

"Well, that's all the information that I needed. You're free to go. It was good seeing you again, Joe."

I was suspicious. "That's all you needed me for? We couldn't have done this over the phone?"

"I never said we couldn't. When I reached out to Tommy, he told me he would get you down here. I just needed your formal statement again."

"Understood, thanks, Detective."

We said our goodbyes and I got back into the Jeep. "How'd it go?"

"Well, it could've been a phone call, but it's fine. I missed it here. How did you find my number anyways?"

"I have my ways." Why did he have to be so mysterious about it? Not wanting to get into an argument, I just left it alone.

"What did you want to do today?" I asked, breaking the silence.

"I have the next few days off, so whatever you'd like to do, we can. I know there are some people who want to see you."

"I just want to hang out like old times, hit a few seafood restaurants, and just be Joe again."

I was relaxed, my name had finally been cleared and my loose ends all tied up.

CHAPTER 33

Sadie

DIDN'T WANT TO BE NEEDY, BUT I HADN'T HEARD FROM LIAM since yesterday when he told me that he was going to be head-down in work. I had hoped that last night he would come back over to keep me company because I didn't want to be alone, but alas, he didn't. I felt like having my house broken into was a big deal that Liam didn't seem to care much about. I figured I would have gotten a text to see if I was alright.

My space had been invaded and no matter how much neurotic cleaning I did, I still felt like I could feel the perpetrator everywhere. The police called earlier this afternoon to let me know that my security cameras had stopped working, so all the files they retrieved were blank. Suspicious, if you asked me. I listened to too many true crime podcasts and watched too many shows to believe that the cameras not working were a funny coincidence. It had to be directly linked to what happened, especially if you added in finding the camera in my bookshelf, the car that sat outside, the weird feelings I'd been having of being watched.

I picked up my phone and texted Liam, asking if he was, in fact, alive and well. No response. I knocked on the door around noon today, but still no answer. Maybe he just had a miserable time this weekend and was avoiding me. I didn't know, and frankly, I didn't care anymore. I tried not to think much about it, but there were certain times when Liam just didn't feel present. When he would zone-out, it was like he was somewhere else because he didn't want to be there with me—maybe he wanted to be somewhere with that Hailey girl. I also thought it was sad how we always eventually ran out of conversation and had to use weird fillers about the weather and other mundane things. This weekend didn't go exactly as well as I had hoped, so maybe it was a sign I should end things. I had my suspicions going to the cabin that it would be a make or break weekend and it certainly was.

I reached for my phone, texting Audrey to see if I could come over.

CHAPTER 34

Audrey

HOW DID YOU TELL YOUR BEST FRIEND THAT THE GUY she was dating is a psycho *and* a murderer? No Google search would help with that. After talking with Kelly Moran, I knew for a fact that Liam wasn't who he said he was. His name was Joe Hale, he was originally from Iowa, and he killed his girlfriend before fleeing Florida and making his way up to Vermont. I knew it was going to simultaneously scare the crap out of her and make her angry that I kept looking into him despite the number of times she told me not to. I needed to tell her soon, because I felt like the break-in was somehow related to Joe and I didn't think whoever did this was done because nothing was stolen.

I saw that I had a message from Sadie.

Sadie: Hey. Are you free tonight?

Audrey: Yeah! I'm ordering in some pizza if you'd like to come over. You can bring Daisy if you don't want to leave her home alone.

Sadie: I'm down. What time?

Audrey: Does 7 work for you?

Sadie: Yep, see you soon!

I wanted nothing more than to tell Sadie that Liam (Joe) was exactly who he said he was and there was nothing weird going on with him. But, that wasn't the case. I knew I needed to tell my life-long best friend that the guy she was dating was a murderer. A real casual night, if you asked me.

I had two hours to kill (no pun intended) before Sadie came over, so I did a little straightening up. I left my notebook on the kitchen island, ready to whip it out when she inevitably lost her shit on me. The anxiety was building, my hands were clammy, my eye was twitching, and I couldn't sit still. The minutes flew by and before I knew it, I heard the unmistakable sound of a key opening the front door, Sadie was letting herself into my house. My stomach dropped while my heart rate went through the roof. It was like being in fifth grade again and having to give a speech in front of all my classmates. I made a last-minute decision to put my notebook away in a drawer—I didn't want her flipping through it before I had a chance to tell her everything myself.

"I'm here!" Sadie called out from the entryway, I could hear the jingle of Daisy's collar bounding toward me while Sadie took off her shoes by the front door.

"I'm in the kitchen," I called back, my voice was shaking.

Sadie came into view, smiling from ear to ear, wearing shorts and a huge T-shirt. I knew her wardrobe, and that shirt definitely wasn't hers.

"What are you so smiley about?"

"Just happy to be out of the house." She sat down at the kitchen island where I was standing.

I nodded.

"So, when are we ordering those pizzas? I'm starving!"

"We can do that now. Small cheese pizza, extra pepperoni?"

"Yes, please." In all the years we've been friends, I'd never seen Sadie eat a pizza that didn't have pepperoni on it in some way, shape, or fashion.

I called and as I was ordering our pizzas, I was fidgeting with the drawstring hanging from my waistband.

Sadie looked at me skeptically and asked, "Are you okay?"

"Yeah, why?" I tried to keep my voice level.

"Your voice was shaky when I got here and now you're fidgeting. Spill. What's going on?"

I paused before answering . . . *Should I tell her now and get it over with or should I wait and see if it comes up in conversation?* The words came out before I could catch them. "We need to talk." My voice was firm.

The concern flashed across her face. "About . . .?"

I inhaled sharply, not sure how to phrase the next bit.

"So, you know how I had some concerns about Liam?"

She cut me off, "Yeah . . ."

"I think I have all of my information sorted and I . . . I don't think he is who he says he is. I can explain, but I wanted to give you a chance to process that first."

Her jaw hung open, her eyes watery. "What? You're kidding, right?"

"Sadie, look . . . I know this isn't what you wanted to hear, but—"

"But what? I told you to stop looking into him. Even if he has a different name, I should be the one to find that out, not you, Audrey."

"I know, and I'm sorry. I just started and then it spiraled."

"After I explicitly told you not to."

"I'm really sorry, I am. I don't know what else to say."

"I'm furious with you, don't get me wrong, but I feel like this is a sign." She started to hyperventilate. I pushed a glass of water her way and told her to take a few breaths.

"What do you mean?"

"This weekend wasn't the best. He seemed to think we had a good time, but there were red flags being thrown left and right and then we came home to the break-in. I've not talked with him since yesterday when he told me that he couldn't come back over. I was coming over here to talk about that."

"Were you already thinking about leaving him?"

"Yeah."

"Well that makes this whole conversation a whole lot easier." I let out the breath I had been holding. "Liam's name isn't really Liam, it's Joe Hale. His dad is most certainly *not* alive and he moved here because he killed his ex-girlfriend Hailey and needed to change his name. Everything has been a lie."

Sadie's eyebrows shot up and she ran to the sink, getting sick.

"I wish it wasn't true, but I have all of the proof. I have it if you wanted to see it." That was the reason I kept it handy.

As she processed what I was saying and washed her face, her eyes welled up. "If this is even remotely true, then why haven't you gone to the police yet?" Her voice shook, a desperate attempt to discredit what I had found.

"Because I didn't want you to get hurt. I knew if I went to the cops before you knew, he could get violent. I wanted you to know first so you could make decisions that would keep you the safest."

"What do I even do now? How do I get out of this without getting hurt or having Liam"—she paused, seeming to catch herself— "*Joe*, suspect a thing? How are we even sure that this isn't just you making connections where there aren't any?"

"Do you want to look at it all?" I pushed the notebook towards her.

"No. Can we just eat our pizza and carry on our night with

some trashy television? I need time to think everything through." She was firm in her answer, unable to make eye contact.

"Of course, we'll take it at your pace." We focused our attention on Daisy, who was there, blissfully unaware something major—and horrible—was happening.

Sadie was taking this way better than I had thought she would.

Our pizzas came a few short minutes later and we ate in silence, both trying to focus our attention on the show playing in front of us, but failing miserably. Every few minutes, I would glance over and see Sadie staring down at her pizza, shifting it around the plate, tearing the crust apart.

After exactly eighteen minutes of awkward silence, Sadie finally spoke up. "How do I have the worst luck in choosing guys?"

"You don't, all guys have some kind of past that they're hiding. It just so happens that this one has a more serious past than the guy with the Rugrats sheets." I tried to console her, but her shoulder shook softly. I knew that I needed to let her cry it out. I excused myself from the couch, going to the kitchen to tidy up, giving her the space she probably needed.

I heard the cries soften and knew this was my cue to head back to the couch. "Can I get you anything?"

"Can you bring the notebook over here, please? I need to take a look for myself."

"You don't have to look at it anytime soon, you can take as long as you need."

"I know, but without it, I will be in denial. Please, just bring it over here."

I obliged, grabbing it off the counter and returning to the couch. I handed it over, and not without hesitation. Sadie had always been so fragile, I was afraid that seeing everything written out would destroy her completely.

Her shaking fingers glossed over the cover of the spiral-bound notebook. "You're sure of this?" she asked.

"I'm as sure of this as I am that we've been friends for a quarter of a century."

I watched her face as she slowly opened up the notebook, taking in the expansive first page of notes. "Shit."

CHAPTER 35

Sadie

HOW DID I EVEN BEGIN TO PROCESS ALL OF THIS? I BEGAN flipping through the notebook, shocked at all the details Audrey was able to find out about Joe (*that* was going to take some getting used to).

"How absolutely certain are you that this is the case?" I asked after going through the notebook no less than four times, not really wanting an answer.

"I wouldn't bet my life on it, but it seems like all the pieces added up."

"I mean, are you sure the pieces don't just add up because you want them to?"

"Why would I want them to, Sadie? What do I have to gain out of this situation?" Her words were sharp at my accusatory tone.

"Nothing, I know. I'm just in denial. I need time. Can I take this notebook home?"

"Why don't you just leave it here, that way if Joe comes over at all, there's no chance that he'll find it." Audrey brought up a very valid point.

I put my coat on and Daisy's leash and said goodbye to Audrey. As we were walking out the door, she stopped us.

"Hey, Sadie?"

I turned around. "Yeah?"

"Please, just be careful. He knows I was looking into him, so I need you to act like nothing is going on until we can come up with a plan to get you out of this safely, okay?"

My eyes widened. "I think you left that part out." I stepped back inside and closed the door. "How does he know that you know?"

"I'm not sure. I'm not a computer genius, but he is, and he mentioned he has some kind of alerts set up to notify him when people searched for his old name? I don't know—he's the computer person."

"How do you know, that he knows, that you know?" That was a tongue-twister.

Audrey's eyes darted down. "He came over last week—on Tuesday, I think. When I saw it was him, I let him in immediately, not thinking anything of it. He practically pushed his way in and verbally assaulted me. He wanted to know why I was looking into him, what I knew already, and told me to stop it before things got out of hand."

My mouth hung open and tears pricked at my eyes once more. "What did you say?"

"I just told him that I knew his secret and that I wouldn't tell anyone, including you."

"But you told me and you plan to tell the police?" I asked, my mind racing a mile per minute.

"Yes, absolutely. We need to get you out of that relationship first and then we can go to the police."

"But what about my house? I live right next to him."

"If the cops get him, then he won't live there anymore. Don't worry, I'm here for you. You and Daisy are welcome here whenever you'd like, you know that."

My heart raced in my chest as we said our goodbyes again and I drove home. I was in such a state of shock, I didn't even remember driving home. I pulled right into the garage, locked all the doors, and started to think of a plan.

CHAPTER 36

Sadie

I woke up this morning still in denial that Liam, the guy I've been dating and possibly loving the last six months, was a potential murderer . . . Well, at least as far as Audrey's research showed. I was holding out hope that it was nothing and there was a reasonable explanation for all of it. I knew he was still over there working or whatever he was doing, so I took my laptop and sat outside, getting some work done on the screened porch. I tried texting him again this morning, still no answer.

I knew what I needed to do, but I had to figure out how to do it safely so he didn't suspect anything before we went to the police. Mid-way through the afternoon, I knew I needed to consult the most logical person I knew: my grandma. I did everything I could to make sure he couldn't hear me. I went into my garage and sat in my car with the doors closed.

"Sadie! How are you doing, my dear?" My grandma's sweet

voice echoed through the phone and I hoped that she would help ease my nerves.

"I've been better. How are you?"

She completely bypassed my question and said, "What's wrong? Are you in trouble?"

I was quiet, so she asked again.

"Sadie, are you in trouble?" Her elderly voice held firm.

"I don't think so. Actually, I'm not sure. Can I come over?"

"Absolutely. Bring Daisy and come on over."

"I'll get ready and be right there."

"Okay, be safe."

I packed up Daisy and drove over to my grandma's house. I pulled into the driveway and I felt a weight lift off my chest—I knew I would find the answers I needed within those four walls. I didn't even need to leash up Daisy, she knew exactly where to go.

Per usual, my grandma was standing at the front door, waiting for me.

"Good afternoon!" she called down the stairs.

I waved from my place on the sidewalk, "Hey."

"Oh, you seem like an unhappy one today." She was extraordinarily observant. Either that, or knowing me my entire life, she knew I wasn't good at hiding my emotions on my face. I was an open book.

I walked up the stairs, trying to figure out how to tell my eighty-year-old grandma that my boyfriend might have killed his last girlfriend and gotten away with it. If all the salt she'd consumed in her lifetime didn't kill her, this just might. My mind started spiraling—should I have even come over here?

"Come inside, you look pale." I felt my grandma's hand on the small of my back. I sat down. "I don't know how to tell you what I am about to."

A cup of coffee was placed down in front of me. "Talk when you're ready."

We sat in silence for a moment before I started. "So, you know how Audrey has had these weird feelings about Liam that she couldn't place?"

She nodded so I continued, "She looked into Liam and he's not who he says he is. She took some convoluted ways, but she found out that his name is actually Joe."

I paused to let her process that information. I looked up, finally making eye contact with her. Her eyes were wide and her mouth was slightly agape.

"Ready for more?"

"Goodness . . ."

I reached for her hand. "And his ex-girlfriend's body was found not too long ago. Liam was suspected of it, but there was no proof, so he was never charged. He likely came here to hide."

She squeezed my hand, a single tear fell onto her wrinkled cheek. It took a minute, but she finally spoke up, "What are you going to do? Are you going to go to the police or are you trying to stay out of his way?"

There was something about hearing her ask me that question that made me start to cry. "I'm not sure. I really came here to ask for your advice. Here I am thinking that I've actually found someone who's worth my time and that I get along great with, but after this past weekend and now this, I can't be happy, once again."

"Sadie," she said as she cleared her throat, "I can't believe I'm saying this, but in order to get out of this safely, if any of this did actually happen, you need to take this slowly. Obviously, you need to be careful, but you don't want him to start suspecting anything. If he does start suspecting something, then that's when things could go wrong, and quickly."

"You really think that I should take things slow? You seem so calm about this—I've been panicking since last night."

"Yes, as much as it pains me to say that." She took a deep breath "I think I'm in shock and I really want you to be safe. You know you can come and stay here whenever. Does anyone else know?"

"No, as of right now, just you, me, and Audrey. I know the police need to be involved, but I'm just worried about him living next to me when they inevitably come to investigate him. What if he does something stupid?"

"More stupid than he already has done?" She paused, this was just a hypothetical question. "How about this: once you feel you or Audrey are ready to go to the police, why don't you drive up and use my cabin? Drop Daisy off here and go take some time for yourself."

I thought on it for a minute, raising an eyebrow. "That would be really nice. I could watch TV or just bring some books and do nothing but read . . . a book lover's paradise. Are you sure you'll be okay with Daisy?"

"Of course! I have this big yard for her to go out and play in. We always have a great time together. You just let me know when you're ready and we'll make it happen."

"I really appreciate it, Grandma."

"Anything to keep you safe. You're very level-headed about all this."

"I'm trying. I guess it's just a combination of things. I'm just still in shock that this is even a remote possibility. At first, I was so mad at Audrey for looking into him, but now I'm thankful that she did. First Ben up and leaves me, now I'm dating a potential murderer . . . how do I have such terrible luck?"

"You don't have terrible luck. There are a lot of bad people out there that trick us into loving them; people that aren't worth our time or our love. Just remember, your main goal while all of this is going on is to remain as calm as possible."

"I'm going to do my best," I said, my heart started racing. "What if I can't go through with breaking up with him? Then what do I do?"

That question seemed to stump her. "You're going to have to get out of it, Sadie Jo. There's not really any other option, you need to start creating some distance. Whether it means you come and stay with me a little bit during the day and make plans with your friends at night, that's up to you. But you have to start keeping busy so you don't have to see him as much."

"Yeah, I know you're right. Can I drop Daisy off later and head up there? I have some client calls I have to take, so I'll just work there and have some time alone."

"Why don't you just leave her here now and bring her food and toys by later? Go take as much time as you need for yourself and don't worry about us!"

That did sound wonderful.

I went home to pack for a few days. I needed this time away, and as much as I hated that I hadn't seen Daisy much this week, I knew she would be in the best of hands. Time away would really help me clear my head and re-focus on myself and what I wanted. Before long, I was packed and organized and on my way. It was only a two-hour drive to my grandma's cabin, so I put on the latest episode of my favorite true crime podcast and drove along the scenic country roads that I loved so much.

The drive was as beautiful as always and the cabin was just as I remembered it—brown and old, yet perfectly homey. I went inside and was met with the familiar smell of wood and must. The walls were still the faded brown wood paneling, the floors creaked when you walked in certain spots, and the once massive-feeling cabin felt a lot smaller than it once did.

I felt the tension in my shoulders melt away. I put my suitcase in the bedroom, turned some lights on, and plopped down on the couch once I had dinner. I wasn't sure what type of peace I was searching for, but I hoped I would find it. I texted Audrey to let her where I was and that my responses would be spotty at best this week, but I would keep her posted on how I was doing.

CHAPTER 37

Audrey

I BELIEVED SADIE GETTING AWAY FOR A LITTLE BIT WAS THE best thing that she could do for herself. She needed some time alone to process all of this information and figure out what she was going to do to keep herself safe. I'd check in with her again tomorrow, just to make sure she was still doing alright, but for now, I was going to take some time for myself and my newly-cleared conscience and spend the evening having a movie marathon—snacks and all.

I flicked on the television and pressed play on my favorite movie, *The Princess Diaries*. I didn't care that I was twenty-eight and watching one of my childhood classics, it calmed me down after the day I had yesterday. Even though my conscience was clear, I still didn't sleep well last night. I fell asleep a third of the way through the movie, but woke up just in time for the final ballroom dance scene. I turned on *Princess Diaries II* and was able to stay awake through all of that. I took this week off from work to go and help my parents finish packing up their house, so I'd been going over in the mornings and helping them and then the afternoons were spent at home doing nothing.

My thoughts went back to Sadie for a moment. I hoped she was alright up at the cabin by herself. I knew she'd lived alone for a while, but she'd never been up to the family cabin by herself. It was out in the woods in the middle of nowhere; granted, there were other cabins around, but still, there was spotty cell phone service at best. If something were to happen while she was outside the cabin and needed help, it would be unlikely that her phone would even work.

CHAPTER 38

Sadie

THE NEXT MORNING, I WOKE IN A MUCH BETTER MOOD. Last night, I was able to start and finish a book in one sitting, then I watched part of a movie in bed and went right to sleep. So now, I was refreshed and ready to take on a new day. I got out of bed easily, sauntered over to where I left my laptop last night on the window bench in the living room that overlooked the trees. I had a client call this morning, so I took it from there and knocked out most of my work for the day. I finished up around three and had the rest of the afternoon and evening to do whatever I wanted.

I reached for the next book in the series I was reading and dove right in, a bag of potato chips hanging out next to me on the couch. Around seven, I got up to make some dinner from the few groceries I brought with me—a box of macaroni and cheese was calling my name. A storm was rolling through, so I was expecting a cozy night ahead. When I was done with dinner and everything was cleaned up, I showered and finished reading my book. It being a thriller novel made me a little more jumpy than usual, and surely, the brewing storm outside wasn't helping me either.

The sky was black, there was a thick cloud cover, and the skies opened up. It had to be one of the most menacing thunderstorms I'd experienced, including the one from a few months ago that knocked out the electricity when Liam—Joe—was over. I heard some rustling outside and tried to brush it off, assuming it was just the wind and some leaves, but the book I was reading had me convinced otherwise. I got up from my spot on the couch and verified that the doors and windows were all closed and locked. When I was by the kitchen window, I saw headlights making their way down the road and broke out into a sweat, no one should have been coming this way at this hour of the night. When the headlights turned in the direction of the next cabin over, I allowed myself to breathe, at least for a little while.

I turned an extra light on in the bedroom and made myself comfortable back on the living room couch. When I was home alone, I was fine, mainly because I knew who was around me and had Daisy there, but now, I was in middle-of-nowhere Vermont, alone in a cabin I hadn't visited in years, not sure of who was living in the cabins surrounding mine. The storm finally slowed to a monsoon and I relaxed, until I heard a rapping at the door. My blood ran cold. All my hair was standing on edge. It was ten o'clock; who could be needing something at this hour?

I grabbed a knife from the block in the kitchen and nervously made my way to the front door. I peeked through the peephole and no one was there. I chalked it up as a tree limb scratching the outside of the cabin, so I put the knife back and resumed the show I was watching, trying to get out of my own head. Between all the weird things that had been happening at home and then the break-in, I was way more on edge than normal.

An hour later, I heard another knock on the door. I waited,

remembering the tree branch from earlier, not in a rush to get up. There it was again, but this time it actually did sound like knocking. I unrolled myself from my blankets and grabbed the knife once again. When I looked through the window, I saw the car that had been sitting outside my house all those months ago and was met with a familiar face. I was shocked.

I opened the door slowly. "I didn't expect to see you, why are you here?"

"You didn't answer my text messages so I wanted to come check on you to see if you were alright."

I put the knife down on the entryway table. "I didn't get any messages, but I'm good. Do you want to come inside? Get out of this storm."

"Why don't you throw a jacket on and come outside with me? The rain has slowed and there's something I saw that I want to show you."

I was skeptical. "What is it?" I asked with a bite.

"A small family of deer were over there eating, I know how much you think they're cute, so come on!"

Even though it was a little out of left field, I still didn't think much of it, I slipped on my rain jacket and headed outside. We walked for almost fifteen minutes before the trees opened up into a massive clearing.

"I thought you said there were deer here?" I was skeptical.

"Hmm, they must have left already. You need to go look out at that view, it's magical, even on a rainy evening."

I was unconvinced, but stepped further out into the clearing, walking toward the edge that overlooked some smaller mountains and streams. It really was beautiful from what I could see in the dark, even on a night like tonight. I turned around to comment and felt a sharp object pressed to my stomach.

"Take off your jacket, Sadie." I did as I was forcefully told, not sure of what was going on, absolutely terrified for this sudden change in character.

The next thing I knew, I was hit with two distinct waves of blinding pain, a pain I had never felt before, and was lying there, alone, gasping for breath. I watched as the shadowy figure walked farther away, leaving me there.

I coughed, and a sanguine taste danced on my lips. I had enough energy to slide my left hand down to my abdomen; it was wet and sticky. I shivered uncontrollably, the leaves crunching beneath my back. My barely-clothed body lying out in the open amongst the trees, leaves cascading down, surrounding me.

When a tree shed its leaves, the leaf died. How ironic that I lay here, dying, amongst them.

I took the remaining energy I had and looked around, admiring the trees; this was likely the final time I would see them. I had no phone with me and I knew that my time was limited. I looked up to the sky as the rain started to fall again, I could hear the car driving away. It all made sense in that moment.

CHAPTER 39

Audrey

I TEXTED SADIE A HANDFUL OF TIMES OVER THE LAST TWO days, but she never responded. I knew she said she wouldn't be as responsive to text messages, but this was a little unusual. She said she was going to be working and reading a bunch while she was there, so that was probably what she was doing. I knew she had a lot of things to figure out, so I left her alone. I probably wasn't her favorite person at the moment either. Even though she'd already been having thoughts of leaving Joe, I was the one who told her that he wasn't who he said he was and that everything he had told her over the last six months had been a complete lie.

She took it *much* better than I had anticipated, but still, I knew she was struggling with it. I gave her another full twenty-four hours to respond before I texted her again.

> Audrey: Sadie, are you okay? I get that you need some time to yourself to figure everything out, but just let me know that you're alright up there.

Four days had now passed since I'd heard from Sadie. I couldn't explain it, but I had a gut-feeling that something was wrong. I called Sadie's mom to see if she had heard from her.

"No, I haven't. Last message I had from her was on Wednesday saying she was doing alright. When was the last time you heard from her?"

"Wednesday as well."

"You sound concerned, Audrey. She was just going to get away for a few days because work had started to pile up, I'm sure she's just fine. You know how the cell phone service is up there."

"Is that what she told you?"

"Yes, it is. Is it not true . . .?" Mrs. Augustine trailed off, almost afraid to finish asking the question.

"Sadie told you that she was swamped with work and that's why she went away for the week?" I needed to confirm the story.

"Yes, that was it." She paused. "Audrey, is something else going on?"

"Mrs. Augustine, can I come over?"

"Of course, dear. I'll be home all afternoon."

"I'll be over soon."

I got in the car and drove over to the Augustine's home, a place I had been in more times than I could count. I rang the bell and Hillary, Sadie's mom, opened the door for me. When I walked through in, the house smelled of apple pie—both mine and Sadie's favorite.

"Would you like some pie? It's fresh out of the oven." My stomach turned at the thought of eating. "I'm good, but thank you."

"This must be serious, you never turn down pie. I even have vanilla ice cream and caramel drizzle."

We sat across from each other at the table, Paul, Sadie's dad, also joining us, and I told them everything.

Paul's jaw dropped when I finished and Hillary's eyes were

overflowing with tears. "So she's in trouble and we just let her go to a cabin by herself?"

"I mean, pretty much."

"And now we've not heard from her in days." It wasn't a question.

"Yes, that's right. I want to call Joe and see if he's heard from her at all."

"Do you have his phone number? Sadie didn't give it to me." Her parents were in full-blown panic mode now, a sob escaping Hillary's mouth.

"I do, Sadie gave it to me to have in case of an emergency." I pressed his name in my phone and let it ring, my hands slipping they were sweating so much.

CHAPTER 40

Liam

AFTER AN AMAZING FEW DAYS ON THE FLORIDA COAST, I was ready to head back to Vermont. Now that everything was sorted out and I had my closure, I felt like I really was ready to start my new life as Liam Reynolds. As I sat on the plane in New Jersey, ready to take off, I thought about how I just up and left Sadie; she thought I was just working next door to her right now, ignoring her in some of her most mentally taxing days. As soon as I got home, I was going to go over there and talk with her. I knew that our little getaway didn't go exactly according to plan because I was side-tracked by this trip I had to take, but I'd make it up to her.

When we landed and my phone had cell phone service again, I had two missed calls from a Vermont phone number—weird, because I didn't give my number to anyone except Sadie. My pulse quickened, what if this was an emergency?

I called the number back immediately and the person picked up on the third ring.

"It's about time you called me back." It was Audrey, her voice was shaky but firm, something was wrong.

"I was . . ." I paused, I couldn't tell her where I really was. "I've been head-down working on this software issue."

"Well, that answers my question."

"What question?"

"If you had spoken with Sadie. Neither me or her mom have heard from her."

"I can go over and check on her now."

I heard a dry laugh from the other end of the phone. "Shows how in the loop you are, she went to a family cabin to decompress for a few days."

"She didn't tell me that . . ."

"Yeah, because you blew her off after you got back from your weekend away. She left two days after that. She needed to be out of the house for a little bit."

"When was she supposed to come home? When was the last time anyone heard from her?"

"She was supposed to be on her way home today, but no one has heard from her since Wednesday. I know that doesn't seem like a long time, but I think I need to call the police to go check on her."

"Why don't we drive up there? How far is it?" I was doing the mental math on how long it would take me to get from the airport to the apartment to get my car, then to drive up to the cabin. I think in passing, Sadie had mentioned it was a two hour drive.

"I would feel more comfortable if we called the local police up there, they would be able to get out there quicker than it would take us to drive there."

"Okay, yeah, that's a good point. Will you call them now and keep me posted?" My heart felt like it was in my shoes.

"Like you even care. You just fell off the face of the Earth after something really traumatizing happened to Sadie."

"I do care! I loved her. It was my fault that she had to go and clear her mind." I paused, realizing what I said.

"Loved?" Audrey's voice cracked. "You loved her? Do you not still *love* her?"

"No, I do. It was just poor choice of wording, I promise." I didn't think she believed me, but it was just a slip-up.

"Yeah, likely story. I just wanted to see if you knew anything about it before I call the police." The line went dead.

I wiped my hands on my shorts, I could read between the lines, Audrey thought I had something to do with Sadie going AWOL. My mind immediately went to a dark place—what if Sadie ventured out and got hurt? What if she was lying somewhere injured and afraid? I couldn't lose someone else in my life—I would have a much harder time getting myself out of this one than the last.

CHAPTER 41

Audrey

I CALLED THE LOCAL POLICE DEPARTMENT AS SOON AS I GOT off the phone with Joe. Go figure, he was no help at all. I made sure to stay with Hillary and Paul so I could keep them up-to-date on everything that was happening.

"Windsor County Police Office, this is Detective Perabo, how may I help you?"

"Hello, my name is Audrey Hayes and I live in Red Oak. I know I'm far away, but my best friend Sadie Augustine is up there in a family cabin and she's not been responding to our messages. Is there any way that you all could do a welfare check?"

"Hello, Audrey. I'm so sorry to hear about this. If you can provide the address, I'll dispatch a car right now." I had Hillary give the Sheriff the address for the cabin.

"Thank you, we will go out and check on her now. Is this the best number to call you back with any further information?"

"Yes, that would be great. And are you in touch with her family?"

"Both her family and her boyfriend."

"Great, can I give you my direct line that way if any of you hear from her, you can let us know?"

I wrote the number down, hopeful that Sadie would reach out to us and this whole situation would resolve itself. I just didn't have a good feeling about this.

Two hours later, my phone rang, Detective Perabo's phone number on my screen.

"Hello?"

"Hi. Audrey?"

"Speaking. Any update on Sadie?" I put the phone on speaker and placed it on the kitchen table so Hillary and Paul could also hear.

"Maybe?" he paused, "I know that's not the answer you were looking for, but she might be just fine. When dispatch got to the cabin, her car was outside and there was no sign of forced entry, which is good."

"I feel like you're going to give us bad news," Hillary spoke up.

"Mrs. Augustine, I can assure you that I don't have any definitive bad news, so that's good. When they went up to the front door, it was unlocked and slightly ajar. It didn't look like anything was taken, maybe she just didn't latch the door all the way when she went out for a walk or something. If you don't hear from her by tomorrow, please give us a call back."

"Can we file a missing person report then?" Hillary and I asked in unison.

"Yes, of course." He took down all of the relevant information needed to open the case and ended the call. Hillary and I were left there, staring at the phone, in silence. What could we do to help this investigation? Detective Perabo had told us to stay put in case she came home, but I knew I needed to do more. I called Joe to relay the news. I couldn't help but feel like somehow, he was involved in all this.

"Audrey? Are there any updates?" His voice was surprisingly worried when he picked up on the third ring. This was probably all part of his act to look like the innocent boyfriend who was concerned. I could see right through it, but for right now, I needed to keep him as close as I could.

"Yeah, a few. I called the police department closest to the cabin. They went out to look for her, but she wasn't there." I figured he would interject here, but he didn't. "They checked the house and her stuff was all still there, the door was just opened a crack, but no one was inside."

"No . . ." His voice was barely above a whisper. I had to give it to him, he was acting the part very well; it was almost believable.

My voice shook. "So, we filed a missing persons case, they're going to keep an eye out."

"We need to do something. I can lead a search party, or hang up fliers, or something. Anything." His voice was desperate.

I stepped out of the room away from Hillary to go outside to the back patio. I couldn't believe I was about to say it. "I'm going to drive up there now and see if I can find her."

"I can come with you," Joe added.

"No, just stay away from her, you've done enough damage." I didn't mean for that to come out.

"What do you mean, Audrey?"

"She didn't have a great time over the weekend. First, you cut it short because you had to work, then you were distant and ignored her."

"She told you all of that?"

"Yes, she did. She tells me everything."

"Oh . . . yeah. I don't have any excuses for that. I was distracted and it ruined the weekend. I need to make it up to her, so we need to start our own search."

"You can do whatever you want to do, but I'll be doing my own thing, thank you. I want you to stay away from Sadie, her family, and her friends. You've done quite enough."

"Audrey, please, just let me try."

"How well did that go for you last time, Joe?" He immediately stopped talking; I knew I struck a nerve with him.

"You're a real bitch, Audrey. You know that? Give me the address to the cabin . . . now." I had angered the beast, probably not a wise move on my part.

"Figure it out yourself." I ended the call.

CHAPTER 42

Liam

NORMALLY, I DON'T LIKE CALLING WOMEN BITCHES, BUT Audrey deserved that. How dare she bring up my past and think I had any involvement with what happened to Sadie. I could never hurt her. How does anyone hurt a person that they love?

Thankfully, I was already home by the time Audrey called me to tell me what the detective said, so now I was closer and could take matters into my own hands. After some sleuthing, I was able to find the address for the cabin. I plugged the address into my phone map app and was on my way to the cabin. I knew Audrey would be there as well, so I was going to do my best to stay as far away from her as possible. I didn't remotely go the speed limit while I was on my way, solely focused on getting to Sadie and making sure she was all right.

The two hours in the car flew by, I must have zoned out. I pulled up to the cabin and Audrey was nowhere to be found, maybe she wasn't here yet. I started out on foot, searching the areas directly around the house; I knew the police had just done it, but maybe an average Joe could see something that they didn't.

I walked around the area for over an hour, still no Sadie or Audrey in sight. I heard leaves crunching behind me as I stood near the car, surveying the area once more.

"Can I help you?" An older man in a police uniform asked.

"Hi, I'm Liam, I'm here looking for my girlfriend Sadie. Her friend Audrey called in the missing person report."

The detective looked me up and down. "I'm Detective Perabo; Audrey told me you'd be here."

"Oh, she did?" I was surprised that she mentioned me.

"Yeah, she did. Mind coming back to the station with me?"

My stomach flipped, I knew what I was going to have to openly admit.

"Please have a seat, Mr. Reynolds." Detective Perabo gestured to the seat across the metal table. I sat down at the table; I was really getting sick of being in these cold, dark interrogation rooms. Here I was thinking that after my stint in Tampa earlier this week, I would be free to start the new life I so desperately craved. I just wanted to go back to a normal life—not one where I was a suspected murderer, but here I was, once again.

"So, how long have you been dating Sadie Augustine?" he asked, looking above his thick-framed glasses.

"Just about six months. May I ask why I'm being questioned right now? Do we know if anything has happened?" I knew he had absolutely nothing on me and couldn't keep me here against my will. I chose to answer some of his questions until they inevitably started becoming accusatory.

"Just trying to gather information, is all." He scribbled something down on his notepad. "Why don't you tell me a little bit about yourself, Liam."

"What do you want to know?"

"Why don't you tell me where you're from, what you do for work, things of that nature."

"I'm Liam Reynolds, I'm originally from Iowa. I moved to Red Oak, Vermont earlier this year and I work in computer science—I'm a software developer."

"Hm."

"Excuse me?"

"Nothing, please continue."

"I answered all the questions you asked me."

"Do you care to elaborate on any of your answers? Maybe tell me a little bit more about your relationship with Sadie?"

"Alright. We're next-door neighbors and didn't hit it off right away, I was kind of an asshole and dismissive at the start. I left her a note and asked her out and the rest is history. We spend a few nights each week hanging out, cooking dinner, and occasionally going out. Cooking together is our favorite hobby—it's stress-relieving and makes us an even better pair. I wouldn't do anything to hurt her, I hope you would know that. I came out here to look for her; to start a search party."

His eyes narrowed. "I think that's all for today. Are you staying nearby?"

"I planned on staying at a hotel up the road."

"Why don't you leave your contact information that way I can call you if I have any more questions."

I left my information. Now that my name was cleared in Florida, I had nothing left to hide.

CHAPTER 43

Audrey

O F COURSE I CALLED DETECTIVE PERABO AND LET HIM know that Joe was going to be up there. I didn't let him know all of the dirty laundry, but I did let him know that I had reason to suspect that Joe was involved somehow in Sadie's disappearance. I could feel it in my bones that it was him—he had done something, I just hoped we found her in time.

Since I knew Detective Perabo was going to confront him, Hillary and I stayed back for a few extra hours to ensure that we didn't run into that encounter. The last thing I wanted was for Joe to know that I called the police on him . . . that would for sure put a target on my back. One that I couldn't have right now.

We packed up the car around eight, once I had confirmation from Detective Perabo that he spoke with Joe, and were on our way. I had to stop and grab an energy drink to keep myself awake during the drive. Hillary was so emotionally exhausted that she fell asleep twenty minutes into the ride. At this point, we were fully convinced that Joe had hurt Sadie and that was why she was missing. No matter how many times he pretended to be a good guy, I just didn't buy it and I knew Hillary didn't either anymore.

When we pulled into the hotel parking lot a little after ten, I wanted nothing more than to check in, shower, and sleep. We collected our keys at the front desk and Hillary told me of her plans since she napped most of the way here.

"How about we both go shower and then we can meet out by the pool and talk about what we can do tomorrow to start looking for Sadie."

"Hill, I think we both need some sleep. Like proper sleep, in a bed. Why don't you call Mr. Augustine and tell him that we made it here safely. As soon as we're up and ready tomorrow morning, we'll drive over and start searching."

"You're probably right. Thank you for driving me here." Mrs. Augustine embraced me tightly, the kind of hug a mom would give her child if it was the last time she would ever see them.

"It was my pleasure." She dropped her arms, so I grabbed her hand. "Everything will be alright, I promise. We will get to the bottom of this as a team."

"I know, you're right. Sadie is so lucky to have a friend like you. Good night, Audrey."

"Good night." We went our separate ways to our rooms.

I opened up the door to my home for the next two nights and it was nothing fancy, but it would do. I grabbed some fresh pajamas and my toiletries out of my bag, headed for the bathroom. I made it in the shower before a sob shook through my body. I put my head on the wall, allowing the water from the faucet to drip down my face, mixing with my salty tears. I knew "Liam" was bad news as soon as I met him; if I would have just told Sadie that his real name was Joe when I found out, maybe she would be here right now. Or better yet, maybe she would be home, safe and sound right now.

By the time I was out of tears, the shower had long run cold. My head barely hit the pillow before I was asleep—I didn't dream all night which was odd for me.

I was woken up by Hillary pounding on my door at seven in the morning; I had forgotten to set an alarm last night. Shit. Covering my eyes with my arm, I went to the door.

"Good morn—oh! You're not ready yet."

"No, I'm sorry. I forgot to set an alarm last night. I think I was asleep before I even got into bed."

"I understand; I set my alarm before we even got out of the car. Go get ready, I'll wait."

I got ready as quickly as I could, throwing on bike shorts and an oversized T-shirt and heading out the door to meet Hillary by the car.

"Ready to go?" I asked, unlocking the car. We got in and drove the ten minutes to the house, a crowd already there. I squinted, driving closer. We got out of the car and walked over to see what the gathering was about. I counted as I walked over, there were already thirty-one people here and at the middle . . . was Joe.

What. The. Fuck.

CHAPTER 44

Liam

I COULDN'T SIT AROUND AND DO NOTHING, I NEEDED TO START looking for Sadie. I created a quick flier yesterday afternoon, made some copies at the copy shop in town, and then hung them up all over town last night. From the looks of it, there were already about thirty people here. I looked toward the back—Hillary and Audrey were here.

"We'll start the search in ten minutes. Thanks, everyone!" I called out before making my way to the duo.

"Hello, ladies."

"Hello, Joe. What are you doing?" Hillary spat.

"Organizing a search party, what does it look like? No one else was doing anything and I couldn't sit around and wait for something to maybe happen," I snapped, shutting them up.

"I was just telling everyone, stay in groups of two or more, be aware of your surroundings, and remember what we're trying to accomplish here. If you see something, say something."

"Where should we go?" They seemed to relinquish control relatively quickly.

I pulled up the map and laid it flat. "You can take section five." I pointed to the northwest section of the map.

"Thank you." And they were gone.

I stayed around the cabin most of the day—just in case more volunteers came out to help. Some trickled in around noon, but then that was it. In all our searching, still no luck. Sadie's car was still at the cabin, so she must have been on foot wherever she was. We kept trying to call her phone to see if someone would hear it, but still nothing.

Around five, my phone was ringing—it was one of the volunteers. I answered as soon as I registered who it was.

"Liam, it's Peter. I think I might have found something."

My heart felt like it was going to explode. "Where are you?"

"Section two, over by the creek, not too far from the house."

"I'll be right there." I called Audrey to tell her that someone had found something. They were going to meet us there. It was a steep walk down to the water, so I could see how someone could easily fall here. We met Peter down at the bottom. As we approached, he pointed down to a sandal. I inhaled a shaky breath and moved in closer. I immediately knew it was hers—on the brown leather strap was the heart she'd drawn in black ink while we were sitting outside last weekend.

"It's hers." I climbed back up to where they were standing. I reached for my phone, "I'm going to call the detective."

"No, don't!" Audrey's voice was firm and broke the silence. We all looked at her. "Let's see if we can find Sadie first, that way it'll be less traumatizing for her."

Odd request, but I could *somewhat* understand what she was saying.

"Let's keep looking." We all spread out again, this time over a smaller area. An hour went by with no luck, until Vanessa, another volunteer started screaming from behind a rock.

"Guys! Guys! Help! Please help!"

I ran to her as quickly as I could. I made it there first, horrified by what I saw. Sadie laid there, lifeless, two stab wounds to her chest. My first instinct was to shield Hillary and Audrey from this. I stopped them before they got there.

"Please, do not go over there. Just call the police. Now!"

"But, please, just let me go . . ." Hillary wanted to see her daughter.

"Hillary, for your well-being, I cannot let you go over there right now. Please just call the police, *now*."

She looked up at me as tears cascaded down her face, and in that moment, I thought she just saw me as another human being who was in pain for the same reason she was. "Okay."

"Audrey, please just take Hillary back to the cabin and get her some water." She nodded in response.

I couldn't bring myself to go back over there, not yet. My heart felt like it had been ripped out and thrown off a cliff—beaten and bruised on its way down. I let myself stand there and cry for a moment, knowing if I didn't, it was going to come out as violence and that was the last thing we needed today. I'd been through this before, and it never ended well for me—especially since I had both Mrs. Augustine and Audrey against me, I had no chance of coming out of this unscathed. I collected myself and knelt next to Sadie; I wanted nothing more than to hug her, hold her, and tell her it would all be okay, but it wasn't.

The Crime Scene Investigation team swarmed the area within fifteen minutes and I stepped back to let them do their job. Audrey and Mrs. Augustine stayed away, answering some questions with Detective Perabo. Even though Audrey was absorbed in another conversation, she kept her eyes on me the entire time, throwing daggers. I wasn't sure what her problem had been with me, but she needed to relax and remember that I was also in shock and grieving the loss of my girlfriend.

Sure, if anyone actually knew the real me, they would certainly be more suspecting, but that was the best part about starting my new life: no one knew who I really was or anything about my past. The fact that my last girlfriend was also missing and her body was recently discovered was pure coincidence.

The pain I felt watching the love of my life be zipped up in a body bag was like no other. While I loved Hailey, the connection Sadie and I had was different. We always had a great time, we loved cooking and doing all of the menial house tasks together, we loved being outdoors and taking Daisy for hikes . . . Daisy, where was Daisy?

I wiped my bloodshot eyes and walked over to Audrey who was now standing alone, watching everything happen; judging by her eyes, she'd been spending her time crying as well.

"Hey," was all I said, hoping that she would be willing to talk for a brief moment.

"What?"

"If you have a second for a question—where's Daisy?"

She shifted her weight to the balls of her feet before inhaling deeply. "She's at Sadie's grandma's house."

I nodded. I could see tears threatening to spill over and handed her a tissue so she didn't have to keep using her sleeve.

"Thank you."

We stood there in silence as we watched the body of the person we both loved be carried away in a bag and be loaded into the Medical Examiner's van.

CHAPTER 45

Audrey

J OE KILLED SADIE, I WAS SURE OF IT. I KNEW EXACTLY what he was doing—he was playing the concerned and heartbroken boyfriend card and I could see right through it. That was exactly why I told Detective Perabo everything. He had Joe in for questioning before Sadie was found, but now that she was dead, he was going to have a whole new set of questions for Joe. What kind of sick person killed not one, but two of their girlfriends? Joe Hale apparently, that was who. At this point, I would do anything I could to help move this investigation along and get justice for both Hailey and Sadie.

Still in shock, Joe, Hillary, Paul, and I were asked to come back to the station to answer a few follow-up questions they had for us. Hillary and Paul answered the questions, then I was brought in next.

"Please, have a seat, Audrey." I pulled out the chair and sat down, a box of tissues were pushed in front of me; I knew I would need them.

"So, tell me about your relationship with Sadie." Detective Perabo got right down to business.

Not even getting the words out, I was already emotional. "We've been friends since we were three. We've done everything together—went to school and graduated high school, went off to college; we even started our jobs on the same day. We've always been inseparable. We used to go on family vacations together. When I say we did everything together, I mean it."

I tried my best to keep myself controlled to answer the questions as best I could, but I had completely lost it and started to bawl my eyes out. I would never see my best friend ever again. We wouldn't be able to go get dinner or get our nails done, go for brunch or talk about work. How do we get in contact with her clients to let them know? My mind raced with all of the things we would have to handle. My heart broke.

"Can you tell me more about why Sadie came up here in the first place? This was a family cabin, correct?"

"Yes, that's correct. Sadie and Joe had gone on a weekend getaway last weekend and he had to cut it short for work." I put air quotes around work because I still didn't believe that he was working. "When they got home, Sadie's apartment had been broken into, but nothing was stolen, the door was just opened, much like the cabin. Joe left as soon as I got there and this morning was the first time we had seen him. Sadie came over to my house to tell me that she was thinking of leaving him. She went to her grandma's house to talk through everything and that's how she ended up here. Her main goal was to figure out what to do and how to do it safely, you know, since Liam is actually Joe."

Detective Perabo nodded as he jotted some notes down on the notepad. "And how long have you known that Liam is actually Joe?"

"A little while."

"And why didn't you tell Sadie?"

I didn't want to have to go through this again. "How do you tell your best friend that the guy she has been dating and loves killed his ex-girlfriend and got away with it? I was concerned for Sadie's safety, and quite frankly, my own. She already had told me to stop looking into him, but I persisted and found what I did. I know she was still frustrated with me, but she was happy that I told her so she could make the decision that was right for her."

His eyes widened, I had said too much.

"Were you ever planning on telling the police?"

"Yeah, we were. The goal was to get Sadie out of the relationship and then we were going to call and talk with them about next steps."

"I see. This gives us something to look into." I would think he would care a little bit more about what I was saying, but he didn't seem to. "I think that's all, thank you for coming in."

"That's it?"

"Yep, that's it. Can you tell Liam to come in, please?"

I got up and left the small interrogation room, signaling Joe to go in. I was baffled by how nonchalant Detective Perabo was when I told him once again everything I knew about Liam/Joe and that he was likely the one who'd murdered our sweet Sadie. I drove back to the hotel and got the notebook out of my bag, fully intending on giving it to Detective Perabo as evidence.

CHAPTER 46

Liam

I KNEW AUDREY DIDN'T LIKE ME, BUT I DIDN'T REALIZE SHE was going to call the cops on me when I showed up to look for my missing girlfriend. I entered the same interrogation room as yesterday and sat in the same uncomfortable metal chair, met with the unwelcoming face of Detective Perabo.

"Hello, again, young man."

"Good evening, sir."

"How are you holding up?" His face softened a little bit.

"I guess as best as I can right now. I'm heartbroken."

He nodded in understanding. "I have some hard questions to ask you and need you to be as honest as possible, alright? We can take this as slowly as needed."

"Alright, I'm ready."

"Let's start with the basics—why did you lie about your name?"

That caught me off-guard. "What?"

"Your name. Why did you tell me it's Liam when it's really Joe Hale?"

I froze. "How did you know that?"

"Audrey might have mentioned it."

I was so careful to not bring up anything from my past, I thought I had built a solid story, a believable one.

Detective Perabo saw the panic all over my face. "It's okay, you can tell me the truth. In fact, the more truth you divulge, the less likely you are to end up with a murder charge tied to your name tonight."

I didn't want to go into details about me, but in order to keep my name cleared, I had to tell the truth. Might as well start from the beginning; my dirty laundry was about to be aired out in this stuffy little room. I took a deep breath and started my story.

"My name is Joe Hale. My parents divorced when I was young—I think I had just turned three—and my mom got custody of me, which she really shouldn't have. After the divorce, she fell into a depressive state and became addicted to drugs and alcohol and I often had to fend for myself. My dad would have been the better choice, but he dropped off the face of the Earth as soon as the divorce was finalized." I paused to choke back the tears that threatened to spill, I could feel the sadness creeping up.

"When my mom passed away, I was sixteen. I was too young to live on my own, but didn't want to go into foster care. So, I did what any kid with no family would do, I ran away. I hitchhiked across state lines to leave Iowa and somehow landed in Florida. I found a group of friends and stayed put, crashing on different couches every night; that is, until I met Tommy. My best friend took me in under his wing and let me move in with him. I got a job at McDonald's, which led me to my degree in computer science. While I was living with Tommy, I fell head over heels for his sister, Hailey. We dated for a few years and one day she went missing. I called the police immediately and reported it. We searched for months, but we were always met with a dead end." I wiped my eyes, the pain I felt in my chest now intensifying.

"I was the main suspect since I was both the boyfriend and the one who called the missing person report in. I was questioned more times than I could count, which is why I'm so calm with this one. I know it reflects poorly, but I've been through this before."

"Was Hailey ever found?" Perabo finally spoke up.

"Her body washed ashore in Tampa a few months ago after three years of being missing. Her body was still somewhat intact, so they were able to do an autopsy and checked for any DNA, but they couldn't find anything. Her case is still cold. As you could assume, when that happened, all eyes were on me again. I quit my job, packed up my bags, left a note for my best friend Tommy that I was moving to Vermont, and left during the night. I know that's not how I should've handled it and it only made things look more suspicious, but earlier this week while I was 'working,' I was in Tampa clearing my name. That's the whole truth. I hope you believe me."

I couldn't read Detective Perabo's face; was he believing any of this, or would I have handcuffs slapped to my wrists here shortly?

"For starters, I know this isn't professional to say, but it sounds like you've been handed a shit hand of cards in life, Joe, and for that, I'm sorry. Can you think of anyone who would want to hurt Sadie? Do you think that this was random, or do you think it could have been a calculated attack?"

"Sir, I don't know. I would hope that no one close to Sadie did this, but . . . yeah, I just don't know."

"You sure seem like you have some thoughts tumbling around in your brain." Detective Perabo pulled his card out from under his notepad and slid it across the table. "If you want to talk and maybe get those thoughts out, just give me a call."

I twisted the card between my fingers, debating on what I should do, knowing that if I divulged the information, there was less of a likelihood that I would end up in jail for a murder I didn't commit.

"I can come back tomorrow. I'll be ready then."

"Of course, take the time you need. We'll be here waiting."

I shook Detective Perabo's hand and left the station to head back to my hotel, knowing that it was going to be my word against Audrey's.

CHAPTER 47

Audrey

I DROVE BACK TO THE POLICE STATION TO GIVE THE NOTEBOOK to Detective Perabo, certain that was what he would need to arrest Joe. I knew they hadn't done an autopsy yet, but I needed the police to know that they needed to be looking into Joe more more than they already were. By this point, it was well after eleven at night and I knew the last thing the police working this case wanted to do was sit with me while I parsed through this notebook, but it had information in it that would lead to the arrest of Joe.

Detective Perabo was still sitting at his desk, head in his hands. "Audrey, what are you doing back here so late?" His eyes were glazed over; it had been a long day for all of us.

"I brought my notebook back for you all to look at. I think there's some information in there that would point to Joe as the murderer. I mean, he had motive, wasn't around, stopped answering . . .."

"Why don't we find a conference room to go talk in?"

"Sure, that's a good idea." We walked into a much more spacious space than the earlier interrogation room. I didn't bother sitting down, I chose to pace while Detective Perabo flipped through the pages.

"Audrey, I know you're really wanting to help us figure out who did this heinous act to your friend, but we already spoke with Joe. He told us everything about himself. He seems to believe that it was you who did this. Would you like to explain why he might think that?"

"Because he's trying to cover for himself! Why would I have any motive in killing my best friend? That's absolutely absurd, I hope you don't actually believe him," I spat. I immediately regretted my attitude, I needed them on my side to be able to now clear my name and get Joe behind bars.

"Why don't you head back to the hotel and get some rest, let us do our investigation. We have a car sitting out there by the cabin keeping watch. I will call first thing in the morning with any updates. Right now, I need you to go home and take care of Mrs. Augustine. Good night, Audrey."

He was kicking me out of the police station. I reached for the notebook to bring it back with me.

"You can leave this with us. You shouldn't have a need for it tonight. I'll have the team look at it tomorrow."

I nodded before leaving. I knew I needed to keep myself together for them to believe me. The drive back to the hotel was maddening, I felt like they weren't taking me as seriously as I wanted them to. They had Sadie's killer right under their nose and didn't even know it. Joe must have caught wind that Sadie was at the cabin and went to visit her. I don't know how the rest of the story played out, but I sure know how it ended: my best friend, lying half-clothed amongst trees, with two stab wounds to her chest. Whoever did this had very accurate precision . . . like someone who had previously killed an ex-girlfriend.

The sound of my phone ringing woke me up, I didn't recognize the number, so I answered it, hoping it was good news.

"Hello?"

"Hi, Audrey, this is Detective Perabo. I just wanted to call and let you know that we've already been over to the cabin this morning—we're testing Sadie's clothes for DNA, checking for fingerprints, and checking the surrounding area now that there's some more daylight for us to work with. Would you and Sadie's parents mind coming back down to the station when you have some time this morning? I've already given her a call."

"Sure, of course. We'll be over soon." I texted Hillary to tell her I would be ready to leave in a few minutes; my heart was racing, what if they couldn't find any evidence to link to Joe? Then what happened . . . a murderer went free again?

We rode in silence on the way to the police station. Before we got out of the car, Hillary paused, eyebrows furrowed. "Do you really think it was Joe?"

"Yeah, I really believe that. I gave them my notebook with all the information that I found, so hopefully they were able to find something in there that would implicate him."

I took a good look at her face—it was red and splotchy, like she had been crying non-stop since we got here. I wish I could show more emotion right now, but I was too focused on getting the person who did this to my best friend. Mr. Augustine was at the cabin, taking some time for himself.

We entered the station and Joe was already there, in the conference room with Detective Perabo and another officer that we hadn't been introduced to yet. Was this it? Was he already being detained?

CHAPTER 48

Liam

LAST NIGHT, I BARELY GOT ANY SLEEP, THE VISUAL OF Sadie's body haunting me. I knew exactly what I needed to do. I got out of bed, got dressed, and came to the police station to talk to the officers about what I think happened. I knew that they would likely not believe me, but I had saved my airline tickets to and from Tampa, so I could provide those if they needed them. I felt like I needed to let them in on my suspicions.

"Liam, it's good to see you. You're here early." Detective Perabo greeted me as I walked in the door.

"Can we continue our conversation from last night?" I knew I needed to get it off my chest before I chickened out. We went back to the same conference room as last night, I was ready to tell my side of the story.

Detective Perabo sat down across from me and passed me a cup of water. I wasn't sure if he was doing it to be nice, to gather my DNA, or maybe both. With nothing to hide, I took a sip. "Whenever you're ready, Liam."

"It . . . means a lot that you're calling me Liam. Once I told you, I figured that you would start calling me by my real name."

"Everyone is innocent until proven guilty, and as it sits right now, there's no evidence against you. If calling you Joe brings up old memories and hinders this case, why would I do that? It makes it harder on both of us."

I couldn't keep my mouth shut. "I think it was Audrey."

His eyes grew wide. "Excuse me?"

"Audrey; that's who I think did this to Sadie."

"Those are serious accusations, you do realize that, correct?"

"Yes, sir, I do. I don't have definitive proof, so I know there's nothing to go on, but could search my messages with Sadie and see if I could find anything." I fidgeted in my pocket for my phone.

"We can get to that in a bit, but right now, I need you to tell me what exactly happened that made you think that it was Audrey."

"She's never liked me. Even from the first time I met her . . . and I know that I didn't make the best first impression, but I tried to be friendly once Sadie and I were dating. On one of our first dates, Sadie told me all about how Audrey tended to get a little over protective of her and did everything in her power to make sure Sadie didn't get hurt. She told me that each time she mentioned a guy's name, the following week she would be inundated by things Audrey found about him."

Perabo's eyebrows shot up at that last bit. "Did Sadie believe Audrey?"

I was surprised, I didn't expect that question. "It seemed like it, well, at least for the most part. A few months ago, Sadie and Audrey were supposed to go out for dinner. They went, but Sadie came home with her food; the only thing she told me was that they had gotten into a stupid argument."

"Was Sadie a confrontational person?" Detective Perabo looked up at me, pen hovering above his legal notepad.

"Not at all."

"Please continue."

"There were a few times that I could remember when Audrey just showed up unannounced at Sadie's place when we were hanging out and when Sadie told her she needed to call first, Audrey got annoyed. I think she was jealous that Sadie didn't want to spend every waking hour with her anymore." I chewed on my bottom lip. "I know this isn't anything to go off, but I just don't have a great feeling about Audrey. I'm sorry for bringing this up."

As the words came out of my mouth, I felt more stupid for even coming here. Who would the police believe—her boyfriend of six months or her lifelong best friend? A rhetorical question, because I knew it wouldn't be me.

"Liam, thank you for being open and honest about this. To you, this might not seem like anything, but this definitely gives us an avenue to start down."

"I know at the end of the day it's my word against hers and you're more inclined to believe her because of my past, but I really do appreciate you taking the time to talk with me this morning. If there's any further information I could provide, please just let me know."

"You've been more help than you know, thank you. Our team will keep you updated if we find anything."

I shook his hand and left the room; I felt like he might have actually believed me, and a weight was lifted off my shoulders.

CHAPTER 49

Audrey

A S SOON AS LIAM WALKED BY, I KNEW HE WAS UP TO something, just by the small smile playing on his lips. Mr. Augustine walked in not too far behind us and enveloped Hillary in one of the most tearful reunions I had ever seen. I entered the conference room without asking, surprising Detective Perabo.

"Audrey. Good morning, how are you?"

"Good morning. I'd be better if I knew why Joe was here again."

"It was just some follow-up questioning that we needed to do. Someone needs this conference room, why don't we go somewhere else?" We walked down the narrow hallway, back to the interrogation room. Little weird, but I chose to not think anything of it.

I sat down in the cold chair, a cup of water pushed towards me. The energy between Detective Perabo and I was different today, he seemed less friendly, more closed off. Whatever Joe told him must have really thrown him for a loop.

"What did you want to talk about? Did you want to look through the notebook with me?" I asked, hoping I could shed some light on the notes in there.

"No, we did a very thorough read through between last night and this morning. Why don't we talk more about why you and Sadie fought at the Mexican restaurant a while back?"

My eyes went wide, how did he know that? I knew I needed to be on the defensive now. "Which fight?"

"The one where Sadie left the restaurant and brought her food home with her. Why don't you walk me through that."

"We got into a silly little fight and she stormed off, we made up, no love lost."

"What was the fight about?"

I didn't want to go into detail, but knew I had to. "I told her that I was doing research on 'Liam.' She didn't appreciate it and then stormed off. It took a little over a week, but we made up and it was fine."

"So Sadie knew you were looking into Liam before you officially told her?"

"That's correct."

"Now, did you look into all of Sadie's boyfriends or just Liam?

"His name is Joe, you need to stop calling him that."

"Young lady, I can call him whatever I'd like. Please answer the question."

"Yes, I did look into whoever she mentioned. She'd been hurt by her ex-boyfriend Ben a few years ago, so I did my best to ensure that it didn't happen again. One guy had been previously arrested!"

"And you don't feel that was an invasion of privacy to the men you were looking into?"

"No."

"Is it true to say that Sadie was aggravated with you for looking into these people she was interested in?"

"I don't think she minded. I helped her dodge some shitty guys."

"Understood. Do you think maybe she would have preferred to find things out on her own?"

"Maybe, but I was willing to help, so she should have been appreciative. I mean, look at Joe! He killed someone and got away with it."

"Audrey, you cannot definitively say that it was him. As of right now, there's no evidence that corroborates your story."

I was taken aback, was he serious? I gave him a notebook of proof and he was tossing it aside.

"You have to believe me, Joe did it! He has motive, he had the time, an alibi—everything lines up. He is just very good at manipulating people to get what he wants."

"I think you should lower your tone. I understand that your friend has been murdered and you're upset, but we all need to work together so we can get justice for Sadie."

I knew he was right, but I felt it in my bones that it was Joe. I was out of proof, so now it was my word against his.

CHAPTER 50

Audrey

I SAT ON THE COUCH, EATING BREAKFAST AND WATCHING THE news. It had been twelve weeks since Sadie's body was found amongst the trees. Daisy went to live with Sadie's parents, and the case had gone cold by week three, but that didn't stop everyone, including the local news stations, from trying. The detectives did all they could, but there were no fingerprints, footprints, or murder weapon; nothing to go on. *I had done a good job.*

I might have still been numb, but she was gone. She wasn't a part of my life anymore. Twenty-five years of friendship was gone with two expertly placed stab wounds to her chest. I guess that's life; people were here one minute and then gone the next. I shoveled the last bite of soggy cereal in my mouth when Sadie's face popped on the television screen, and the news anchor started talking. I raised the volume.

"Sadie Augustine was a bright light in our little town. She was a beautiful soul with a creative brain, designing logos and marketing collateral for some of the biggest companies in Silicon Valley. Sadie was beloved by everyone, which is why her death has deeply hurt us. If you have any details about this case, please call our Emergency Tip Line, and someone will be more than happy to take your call. Any person to bring forth information that leads to the capture of her murderer will receive a $25,000 reward, courtesy of her community." The news anchor wiped a tear from her eye. I couldn't tell if it was genuine or not. Knowing the emotional hold Sadie had on everyone, it probably was.

I looked at the banner on the bottom of the television screen. "Sadie Augustine: Case is cold, No proof." My eyebrow raised involuntarily, and a half-smile played on my lips.

"Good."

CHAPTER 51

Liam

I SAT ON MY COUCH, WATCHING THE MORNING NEWS, THEY were covering Sadie's case again. It had been cold for over a month, and, statistically speaking, if nothing was discovered within the first forty-eight hours, then the likelihood of finding anything was slim. This whole situation had me nauseous.

A news anchor appeared on the TV, telling viewers that the community was still mourning Sadie and searching for her killer. There was mention of a hefty reward before the screen cut to another story. I had to give it to them, the little town of Red Oak was doing its best to bring justice to Sadie's situation.

Staring blankly at the television, I wondered where I went wrong. My plan was fool-proof, immaculate even; I had my sights set on Sadie for over a year and had everything going according to it, then Audrey had to get involved and unravel my past. She couldn't just leave it alone. I knew she was the one who killed

Sadie, that was obvious, well, to a trained eye like mine. Yes, I killed Hailey.

Now with Sadie gone, I guess it was time to try this again. I heard South Carolina was a nice place to live—lots of beaches and even more remote marshland . . . perfect for disposing of bodies.

THE END.
For now.

ACKNOWLEDGMENTS

I don't even know where to start with my thank you list. Should we cue the Oscar's music when I start getting too long-winded to usher me away from the podium and microphone?

Ross, thank you for dealing with my incessant talking about this novel. If we had a dollar for every time, I said, "I'm up to page X," we would be millionaires and I would quit my job and be an author full-time. Thank you for dealing with all my random questions; "What do you call what men swim in?" "Would you call that an airport convenience store?". Sorry for blowing your mind repeatedly throughout this writing process. I promise none of the characters in this book are modeled after you.

Mom and **Dad**, thank you for always supporting my book addiction and my dreams. Without the countless trips to Barnes and Noble and Books-A-Million, I wouldn't have developed a love of reading, which has translated into writing. No matter what I choose to do in life, you're both always there, cheering me on and helping me live my dreams.

My **beta readers** and the **Bookstagram community**, you all are the real MVPs. You've let me bounce ideas off you, have given valuable feedback when I'm torn about something, and are some of the biggest cheerleaders I've ever met. I'm so incredibly grateful for every one of you beautiful human beings. Who knew that creating an Instagram account would've brought me my tribe.